THE LITTLE GREY MAN

Identical twins Jerry and Harold Mills are polar opposites. Jerry, hardworking and reliable, has made a success of his life and is engaged to the beautiful Andrea. But his brother soon exhibits his criminal nature and is forced to flee the country and disappear. Five years later, now a murderer and fugitive hiding in Marseilles, Harold writes to his brother, begging him for help. But when the brothers meet, Harold murders Jerry and assumes his identity, faking his own suicide. Then he returns to England, and Andrea . . .

NORMAN FIRTH

THE LITTLE GREY MAN

Complete and Unabridged

LINFORD
Leicester

First published in Great Britain in 1947

First Linford Edition
published 2014

A catalogue record for this book is available
from the British Library.

ISBN 978–1–4448–2195–6

Published by
F. A. Thorpe (Publishing)
Anstey, Leicestershire

Set by Words & Graphics Ltd.
Anstey, Leicestershire
Printed and bound in Great Britain by
T. J. International Ltd., Padstow, Cornwall

This book is printed on acid-free paper

1

The Legionnaire

They brought Harold Mills his sparse meal of bread and gruel at the usual time. Then they left again, leaving only the guard to watch the punishment cell.

There was only Mills in it; he was facing court martial for desertion. And the Foreign Legion have a notoriously short way with their deserters!

Mills ate the food ravenously. He was going to need it to face that which he had to face. And having eaten, he peered from the tiny slit in the stone cell at Fort Haroun, and noted that the light had gone, and the moon had yet to rise.

He had but a few minutes to spare; it was *now or never!*

He put the first part of his plan into operation.

'Guard — *mon ami* . . . '

The guard wasn't a bad-natured man

at heart; he was a Swede, had fled from his country after murdering his wife's lover, and had wound up in the Legion, like many of its recruits. He came down, stood his rifle by the wall, and said, 'What is it you want, my friend?'

Mills lowered his voice and whispered, 'They took from me my cigarettes. And my tongue is hanging out for a smoke — you know how it is, eh?'

The Swede pursed his lips; he knew how it was. Even though the only cigarettes obtainable out there tasted like camel droppings, they helped a man to keep his sanity. He said, 'Just a minute while I see if anyone there is about.'

He went along to the outer door and stared across towards the barracks, a black bulk in the black desert silence. He could hear a rattle of mugs and shouts of laughter. There was cursing, too, and Little Slim, the Yank, was playing his harmonica. Everything seemed normal enough.

He foraged in his white cap, produced a battered paper packet and slipped out one of the thin brown cigarettes. He went back and handed it through the bars to Mills.

'Thanks — got a light, Swede?'

Olsen nodded. 'But be careful, Mills. It only just needs the sergeant major to come round and see you smoking, and by jiminy, I'm for being on a charge at the same time as you! Here.'

He struck a match and leaned close to the bars, cupping it with his hands. His face was hardly ten inches from the prisoner. His chin was half turned away, watching the outer door.

Mills got a lot of power into the blow: so much power that the good-natured Swede staggered backwards across the passage, and his head whammed hard and sickeningly against the far wall.

He was out — Mills had made sure of that. Mills lay full length and reached between the bars. His fingers came two inches short of the Swede's foot, even when his arm was fully extended. He cursed and struggled furiously to force his arm farther through the bars.

No use! The Swede might have been a million miles away as far as the sweating

Legionary was concerned. And at any moment the sergeant major might come on his rounds!

A sudden hope struck Mills, and frenziedly he tore off his tunic, formed a loop in one of the sleeves, and tied a knot to hold it firm. Then he edged it through the bars and slid it slowly over the Swede's upturned foot.

It lodged there, and he began to ease it back, gently. The Swede moved a few inches closer; he discarded the tunic and reached out, dragging the man parallel with the bars. It was simple then to unhook the key, fit it to the lock, and open the door. He threw the Swede inside, and something about the feel of Olsen made him peer closely —

Olsen *wasn't* unconscious! He was *dead*!

That crack on the base of the skull as he had hit the wall had done the trick!

Mills grunted to himself. 'Poor swine's better off dead anyway. If he'd lived they'd have flayed him alive for letting me escape!'

Then he tensed. He could hear the dull

thud of heavy boots crossing the square, heading for the prison block. Quickly he grabbed the rifle Olsen had discarded and slunk behind the door that led out into the square. If he was caught now — what with the Swede and everything — there could be only one outcome. He'd face a firing squad — after they'd flayed every inch of skin from his back under the blazing sun!

He mustn't be taken!

The door swung open and the hated, black-jowled sergeant major strutted in with his usual pomposity. Mills held tight, back of the door —

The sergeant major exploded, 'What the *hell* — Olsen, you *cochon*, you name of a pig, where are you?'

He noted the sprawled figure in the cell. He took a step forward and Mills swung the butt of the rifle outwards.

It hit him in the face, just above the chin. It carried all the weight of Mills' arm behind it, and it didn't even give him a chance to cry out. He went down and stayed down, and Mills grated, 'I hate your guts! Hang on to that, too!' and dealt him another forcible blow across the face with the rifle butt.

Then he was out of the prison block, running across the dark square, to the east wall. There were sentries at the four wall turrets of the fort. But they were careless. There hadn't been an Arab rising for six months. They didn't think there might be danger *within* the fort. And so they didn't see as Mills grovelled the sand away beneath a chipped stone of the wall, forking in there until his hand closed on a tight roll of waterproof skin.

That was the money — the money he'd saved ever since he'd joined the Legion five years before. And he was going to need every sou of it to make good his escape!

He stuffed it into his pocket. He grubbed about again and brought out a coil of thin rope, which he had brought back with him on his last visit to the village of Ag-el-Zatun, which lay three miles north of Fort Haroun. He'd brought it back wrapped round his body, together with a long Arab robe as worn by the poorer classes. He'd hidden them here with his money in the sand, against his desertion. He shoved the robe down his tunic. No use donning it yet; it would only hinder his activities.

He walked along to a point where a flight of stone blocks led up to the eastern firing ramp. They brought him to the wall top about thirty yards from the guard posts at either end. Working rapidly, he made a loop in the rope and tightened it over one of the cover blocks on the wall.

The moon came out and cast a pale radiance over the fort and the desert. The sands gleamed silver in its rays. Mills held his breath and crouched low, hoping the guards would not be on the alert. There were two sentries at each post — and usually they played cards once the sergeant major had made his rounds.

There was no alarm; rapidly he tested the rope, then lowered himself by its aid. He slid down about twenty feet of it, then found it terminated abruptly. He still had ten feet to go.

He chanced the drop, landing on hands and knees. Then, taking advantage of the undulating sand dunes, he hurried out into the desert, taking a course which would bring him — he hoped — to Ag-el-Zatun.

★ ★ ★

The Café of the Lone Camel in Ag-el-Zatun was doing its usual business. A motley assortment of Arabs squatted cross-legged on the floor. Those more fortunate sat about the small bamboo tables.

They smoked and talked, the buzzing of their voices rising above the wailing of the reed orchestra in the corner. They drank sweet coffee, and ate sweet cakes, and whilst they talked their eyes watched, through the haze of blue smoke in the room, the convolutions of the girl who was dancing in a small, clear space in the centre.

She was Eta; she did not know her other name. Her mother had been a low-caste Frenchwoman, her father a low-caste mixed-race Arab. Strangely enough, the product of their union was small and dark and lovely. Her taut brown body wriggled and writhed to the tune of the reed pipes. Her sole covering was a small girdle which circled her waist, and from which hung tenuous strands of silk. She danced in a circle, caressing the bearded faces of the lusting sons of the sand. But she was too elusive for their grabs to draw her to them.

The Arab didn't seem to know his way around too well. He came into the Café entrance and stood gazing inside before he took the plunge. Then he almost slinked in, trying to make himself as inconspicuous as possible. No one took very much notice of him. If his skin was a lighter texture than usual, what matter? There were many half-castes, offspring of an amalgamation between French and Arab, in that vicinity. And to disguise his pale-ness as far as possible, he kept his burnous drawn low about his face, and gathered in to each cheek.

He chose a solitary spot beside the end of the reed players to sit. He sat awkwardly, as if unused to falling into the cross-legged position so natural to the native element. He sat and waited.

The turnings of Eta's dance brought her before him; she stooped and stroked his smooth-shaven face softly, voluptuously. He said, in a voice that was almost a whisper, and could be heard by no one but Eta, '*I need your help . . . Ali Abram sent me.*'

Eta gave no sign that she had heard his words. The dance drew her away and her eyes left him and did not return. He sat on, waiting. It was all he could do now.

If she failed him . . .

The dance finished to riotous yells and laughter, and lewd remarks on Eta's undeniable charms. Eta smiled, kissed her hand, and ran daintily behind a curtain at the far end of the room. The reed players struck up another dirge and conversation recommenced.

The lone Arab sat perfectly still where he was, unnoticed by the others. Two legionnaires from a nearby unit jested and mauled Arab girls in a small alcove. He kept his face turned from them.

A native glided from the curtains behind which Eta had so recently vanished. He came towards the lone Arab and stopped.

'Eta wants to see you. Come.'

The Arab picked himself up, and with many guilty glances at the Legionaries walked after the native behind the curtain. No one even noticed his going. Many men had business with Eta behind that dark curtain. And it was unwise to enquire into that business too closely. Tales there were of men walking home through the night, and being found later with knives buried in their backs. Tales too of men who had found poisonous snakes and spiders in their beds. Tales of men who had found *unusual* ingredients in their broth. All had died the death. All had been too inquisitive about Eta and her affairs.

Eta was waiting for him in a small room off to the side. She was wearing nothing more than a gauzy robe of some material, and despite his plight the heart of the man raced, and the blood of the man began to pound in his veins. Eta said, 'If Ali Abram sent you, you are a Legionnaire, yes, *m'sieu?*'

The man nodded and threw back his burnous.

2

The Letter

He nodded as she studied his face. He said, 'I bought this robe and some rope from Ali Abram — he told me that *you* would help me . . . '

'You are deserting, *mon ami?*'

'I *have* deserted. I tried once before and — they took me back. Tomorrow I was to have stood trial . . . '

'They would have flogged you?'

'Or *worse*. Can you help?'

'From which post are you?'

'The fort at Haroun. Three miles away. Ali Abram told me you could get me back to French territory . . . I mean right out of the desert altogether, Marseilles or somewhere else. Can you?'

'Did Ali Abram tell you how much this would cost?'

He took the roll from his pocket and said, 'All of this except one hundred francs. I need that — to help me — until I can arrange something.'

'You *can* arrange something? Have you friends?'

'One brother — in England. He is my twin.'

'And you can contact him from Marseilles?'

'I hope so. If you can get me there.'

She became very brisk. She said, 'Tonight you will stay with me . . . '

'With *you?*'

'I like Englishmen, *M'sieu*. And there is a cellar beneath this house where you would never be found should they search. All the men I help to escape stay there until things are prepared. Tomorrow night you start your journey for Marseilles.'

'You're sure they won't *find* me?' he said, hesitantly.

She laughed. 'They will not find you, *chéri*. And you will not be *bored* by your voluntary imprisonment — Eta will see to *that!*'

★   ★   ★

Andrea Marsh gazed up from her coffee and toast, and said, 'What *is* it, Jerry?'

'Eh?' Gerald Mills lowered the letter he had been reading and looked at her. His face was lined with worry — an unusual thing in the usually light-hearted Jerry.

'I said what is it? You seem so worried about something. Of course, I'm only a guest here . . . '

'Don't be silly. You're as much at home as I am. In another few weeks we'll be married, and then this *will* be your home. Meanwhile you may just as well get used to it.'

'Anyway,' she smiled. 'I couldn't help noticing how worried you look. Sorry you asked me to marry you, darling? And — even sorrier I said *yes?*'

He crossed over to her, bent, and kissed her on the lips. He said, 'Don't be an idiot, Andrea. You know I was never happier about anything in all my life!'

She looked puzzled. 'Then what on Earth's making you look like the Lord High Executioner?'

He frowned again and picked up the letter. He seemed uncertain just how to start. At last he said, 'You've heard me mention my twin brother often, haven't you?'

She nodded. 'You never said very much about him though.'

'I know. You see, if you were to open our family closet, he's the *skeleton* that'd tumble out. We all thought he was dead . . . it's more than five years since he was heard of . . . but, as you're due to marry into what bit of family I've got, you'd better know it all from the beginning. Then — you can back out if you feel inclined.

'Mother and father both died when Harold and I were five years old. They died in an automobile smash. We didn't feel it because we were young enough to forget quickly; and too excited at the idea of being brought up by Uncle Jim, whom we'd always liked, to worry much. We were — or I should say we *are* — twins, Harold and I. But I'm afraid I'm not by any means proud of it!

'When we came of age, with the money Dad left, I went into the chain store business. I'm still in it as you know, and doing very well. Harold, as the eldest — by an hour as a matter of fact — took over Dad's business, which Uncle Jim had kept running. Dad, as I've told you, was a stockbroker.

'To cut it short, Harold started embezzling. The money he was entrusted with went on gambling and wine and women. In the end he came to me and told me the hole he was in — had to find five thousand pounds by a certain date, or he'd had it.

'I was only just finding my feet. I couldn't have laid hands on five hundred. He knew Uncle Jim wouldn't help him — you can understand that having seen Uncle Jim yourself! — so at last he begged enough from me to clear out of the country.

'That was the last I heard of him: he went to France and he'd vanished utterly, long before the thefts were discovered. So Uncle Jim took over the firm and kept it running, making the losses up from his own account.'

Andrea said, 'Must say I think he did the wisest thing by clearing out. But why bring that subject up *now?* You know that doesn't make an atom of difference to *me!*'

Jerry smiled. 'I know, dear. But — this letter I have here is from Marseilles. And it's from *Harold!*'

She started, and took the letter he offered her. She said, 'I'm not sure I should, Jerry . . . '

'It's all right. You're almost one of us already, Heaven help you. Go ahead and read it.'

She opened it and read out. 'My dear Gerald, I expect you will get quite a shock when you open this letter and find it's from your devoted brother, *Harold!* Of course you will. I daresay you thought — no, *hoped* is the better word — that I was dead and buried, after the way I smirched the family escutcheon. You always did tend to be a sanctimonious prig, in *my* opinion. I remember that lecture you gave me when . . . but skip it.

'Fact is I need help — and badly! I've been in the Foreign Legion for these last five years. And I don't mind saying I wish I'd stayed home now and taken the sentence. It's been Hell, that's the only word for it that I can use without offending your aestheticism.

'Now I've deserted!

'All right, Jerry, don't raise your hands in shocked horror. Even the bearer of the noble Mills name couldn't be expected to stay with a herd of filthy pig-dogs any longer than it took him to save enough to buy his passage to liberty.

'I need help — and *you* have to give it to me! Will you? *Of course* you will, you fool! You won't think twice about it. You'll come running over here like a scalded hen to give me any help you can, and another lecture, *despite* what I may call you in this letter. You'll *come* — but you'll be annoyed. You'll come because there's a tie between us stronger than the tie between ordinary brothers — because I'm part of you, Jerry, just as you are part of me!

Come to the address on this letter — but be careful. You will find me there — not a *pleasant* neighbourhood; it's smelly and down by the docks where the big ships sail from, but if you hold your immaculate handkerchief to your aristocratic nose you'll just about survive. You're lucky; you'll only have to pass through it. I've had to *live* in it for *weeks!*

'Hurry up. My money's getting short, and there're a hundred men round here who'd sell me for a lousy franc. Bring plenty of filthy lucre with you, *and leave your sermons at home*!!! Harold.'

She set the letter down and stared at Jerry. He said, 'Well?'

'You won't go, Jerry? His letter's positively insulting. I don't see how he could *expect* you to take any notice.'

'He knows me — he knows me better than I know myself. I have to go, Andrea. I couldn't sit here in luxury and think of him living in some smelly, flea-ridden haunt of vice along the waterfront at Marseilles. He's right — I'll go!'

'But — *Jerry* — '

'It won't delay the wedding. I'll be back in lots of time.'

She reflected a moment. Then, 'It won't matter — because I'm coming *with you!*'

He jumped, then took her by the

shoulders and said, 'Oh no, you're not! You aren't getting mixed up with this dirty business. I wouldn't dream of it. He's my family, and I'll take care of him without any outside help.'

'But darling, you just said a moment ago that I was as good as one of your family . . . so . . . '

Jerry grinned and said, 'Just like a woman, shooting something like that at a man. But it doesn't matter *what* you say — *You're not being entangled in this mess!*'

Andrea pouted. 'I bet the truth is that you want to have a last fling before you tie the unhappy knot,' she chided. 'I expect you'll get up to all sorts of no good with those French trollops. In fact I wouldn't be at all surprised if you hadn't sent that letter to yourself, simply to get away from me!'

He laughed. 'Now how did you guess?'

She stood up with a smile and put her arms about his neck. She drew his lips to hers and murmured, 'You *are* going to take care of yourself, darling? Remember, you're all I've got.'

He returned her kiss and said, 'The same applies the other way round. Don't worry, Andrea — I won't take long. And while I'm away you can get around with young Arnton . . . you have my permission.'

She said indignantly, 'Young Arnton's the worst type of wolf. You'd actually surrender me into *his* hands?'

He grinned. 'He's my friend . . . and I thought you rather liked him?'

'I do like him — always have. But you know what they say about never introducing your donor to a friend . . . '

'That doesn't matter. You know him already.'

'Hmm. Well, if he suggests a quiet bit of supper at his flat, I'll flatten his nose for him. How's that?'

They laughed, and then Jerry went inside to telephone for a boat reservation, and to start packing. He meant to leave at once. Things like this wore him down if left in the air, and he'd have to hurry to get back in time for his wedding.

When he had gone in, Andrea picked idly at a flower on the terrace, poured herself another coffee, and looked rather worried. Her reverie was broken by a tootling motor horn in the drive, and she became aware of Barry Arnton: young, dark, and good-looking. He came over to her and said: 'I say, Andrea, have you two chumps forgotten we were driving to town together today?'

Jerry came out of the house and said, 'Managed to get a berth on the midnight boat — oh, hello, Barry. Just the man I want. I'm going away for a few days, and I'll need *you* to take good care of Andrea.'

Barry stuttered, '*Going away? You — oh, good!* Maybe I'll be able to cut you right out with Andrea before you get back!'

Jerry laughed and said, 'If you try it, Andrea's given me her word she'll flatten your nose — so you'd better arrange to have a good plastic surgeon on hand, Barry!'

3

Treachery

Harold Mills took another drag at the limp cigarette between his twitching fingers, and polluted the atmosphere of the tiny room he was in by some plain and fancy cursing. It helped to relieve his feelings.

The room was in a dirty house, let into quarters for seafaring men and less desirable characters, in a filthy street in the black heart of the dock area of Marseilles. The rent was low and questions weren't asked. The other tenants minded their own business and left you to mind yours.

He had been there eight days, and it was eight days too long for his liking. The Legion had accustomed him to terrible conditions, but even so he had nothing like this to face, even in the formidable Fort Haroun, the dread of every Legionnaire.

Eight days!

He wondered if Jerry had received the letter he'd sent some four days previously, and if so how long it was going to take for Jerry to get out to him. Perhaps — perhaps Jerry had received the message, but had no intention of coming to his aid? Perhaps Jerry had changed in the last five years? Perhaps Jerry was — *dead!* He had no way of knowing. He could only hang on and wait, and hope, and sweat and smother in the foul air which never left the building, in the narrow room where the fleas played leapfrog with the cockroaches, and which he dared not leave.

No food, now. He'd spent his final cent the day before. He'd got rid of most of his money on a suit of cheap blue serge and a roll-necked sweater. His Legion clothes were rolled up and stowed away in one corner together with the Arab garb. Eta had seen he got to Marseilles by dint of much smuggling, but the money he'd paid her hadn't covered a new outfit for personal wear. That he'd had to pay for himself.

He swung a leg to the floor and opened

the door. He looked along the shabby corridor. There was a girl cleaning up there. She was the half-caste Roella, whom the owner of the place paid to keep the passages in some sort of order, and generally do the dirty work.

She looked questioningly at him as he stared at her. She was dirty and untidy, but there was a sexuality about her little figure. And Mills wasn't particular.

'You busy, Roella?'

'No sah.' She knew what he implied.

It was hardly five minutes later that there was a tread on the stairs, and Jerry Mills came along the landing. His open, honest face, so much like his twin brother's, expressed disgust. He hadn't expected his precious brother to fall quite so low, whatever the circumstances!

He took off his light hat and mopped his forehead with a spotless handkerchief. His nose wrinkled as the unpleasant odour of poor cooking and stale human bodies met it. He wiped his fair hair back into position and found the door he wanted. He knocked.

Harold opened the door, and seeing

who it was, stood aside to admit him. There was no exuberant greeting between these two men. Any affection they had had for each other had long ago faded and been destroyed as a result of their widely differing natures.

Jerry walked in — and stopped. Harold said, 'Get out now, Roella.' He turned to Jerry: 'Got any money handy?'

Without a word Jerry handed him a note. He turned and threw it to the half-caste girl, who was leaving.

'Thank you, sah. Roella come later?'

'Maybe.'

She went out.

Harold had not spoken yet to his brother, other than to make the request for money. Now he said, 'Well, my *dear* brother. So you came.'

'I came — God knows why, but I always did when you were in any trouble.'

'You always were *noble*,' sneered Harold. 'I presume you came with the money?'

Jerry nodded. 'I thought you'd sunk low *enough*, to stay in a place like this — but — that — *that girl* — how the devil *could* you . . . '

Harold sneered. 'After five years with the Legion, one gets used to unsavoury smells — *and* women.'

'You deserted from the Legion, you say?'

'True. I besmirched the family honour — again. And no doubt I'll do the same a great deal in the future. But right now the most important thing is for me to get to South America, my dear brother. Out there I'll be safe — '

Jerry snorted. 'Why don't you be a man for once? Why don't you get back to the Legion and take your punishment for desertion, and serve your time out? Then you can come back to England . . . '

'Wouldn't you *like* that?' mocked Harold. 'I don't think. No, my devoted brother, it isn't so easy as all that. If I give myself up — or if they recapture me, there'll be only one outcome. You see, it so happens that I killed one man in my escape. Hit him too hard, and he cracked his skull on a wall. For all I know I might also have killed the sergeant major too. So it isn't quite practical for me to give myself up.'

Jerry had started back and was looking

at him with horror. He said: 'You — you're a *murderer?*'

Harold shrugged. 'No need to be upset about it. It isn't as if they *counted.* They were both no-good scum like myself. Human life doesn't count for much in the desert, Jerry. There's a very *different* set of values in operation. Most of the Legionnaires are living on borrowed time anyway. Most of them would be sentenced to death by their respective countries if they could be found. They're a bunch of murderers and cut-throats!'

'That doesn't excuse you. Your up-bringing . . .'

Harold sneered. '*Upbringing!* There you go again! You and your damned snobbery. Haven't I told you before, it isn't how you're brought up but what's inside of you? Haven't I argued all that out with you? If you're weak you naturally drift along the path you've been taught to drift along, obeying a set of outdated commandments which don't count for anything anymore . . .'

Jerry stated grimly, 'They still count to *decent* people.'

'Decent people,' grunted Harold. 'God,

what a shock it'd be to see into the minds of some of those *decent* people of yours! How about the tired businessmen who go to see a leg show? If you could strip them of their sham you'd see a roaring atavistic ape who'd rape and pillage and plunder. It's all there underneath; but they hide it by the outward veneer of culture and convention. They lead the lives of prisoners . . . prisoners in a cage of the morality they pretend to uphold, and secretly hate!'

'Who's sermonising now?'

Harold shrugged. 'The money? How much did you bring?'

With an expression of disgust, Jerry took out his wallet and threw it onto the truckle bed. Harold picked it up and looked inside it, then said: 'Is this *all?*'

'It's enough for you to get to America . . . and that's all I intend to give to you. I won't give you anything to spend on your wretched depravities. If I did as I should I'd turn you in to the police right *now.*'

Harold sat down on the edge of the bed and nodded to the single rickety chair the room boasted. 'Sit down, dear brother. Tell me how you're getting along now.'

'I don't think we can have very much to discuss together,' Jerry told him stiffly. 'Our circles are widely different. I'm sure I don't care to hear the details of your revolting life, and I don't expect you'd get a big kick out of the details of my priggish one, as you call it. If you're a sample of what unconventionality does to a man, by God, I'm glad I'm *conventional!*'

Harold said, 'I don't intend to dirty your nice clean mind by a recital of my own loose living, brother. But I am interested in you and your affairs; don't forget that I was brought up in England, the land of my birth, and low though I may have sunk I have still retained a great deal of affection for it. So just forget what an objectionable person you're talking to, and tell me how the business is, who your friends are, if you're married, and all the rest of it.'

Hoping to drag him back some way from the edge of the pit of rottenness he was standing on, Jerry told him. He talked for a long time, with an occasional question from Harold. He told him of the firm, of how the business was prospering, of how he had opened eight more branch stores, and where they were. Then he told him of the new house he now occupied, and of how it was shortly to serve as a home for himself and Andrea.

'So you're getting married?' said Harold slowly.

'I am — another week.'

'What kind of a girl is she? One of the dull, stuck-up English aristocracy?'

'I'd rather not discuss her with you,' Jerry told him frankly. 'In fact I hardly think you're fit even to speak her name!'

Harold grinned and said: 'Going all noble again, brother?'

Jerry got up and said, 'You have the money — I can see that all the talk in the world won't light a tiny spark of decency in your dirty corruption! I'll be going . . .'

'I see. Running away from me now, eh? Afraid your blasted purity'll be sullied by contact with such a disreputable person as your brother's become?'

Jerry turned and looked at him, then said, 'The only thing that might do you any good would be a damn good *flogging!* You *need* it!'

'Do I, blast you?' mouthed Harold viciously.

31

'Then let me inform you that *that* wouldn't do me any good, even. *Nothing* would. I've got my own standards and I'm going to live by them. And I'll lay even money I live longer than *you, and* have more fun. And if you think *physical pain could change* me . . . here, take a look at *this*, and you may understand that when a man's been through something that sears his whole soul as much as *this* does, he doesn't give much of a damn what he does to *others!* Go on, you blasted prude, feast your sanctimonious eyes on it!'

He wrenched suddenly at the back of his damp shirt, hauled it off, and turned his back to his brother. He sneered. 'Pretty, isn't it?'

Jerry could only stand and stare at the red, angry, half-healed criss-cross of scars on his brother's back. Scars made by some flailing lash or whip, which had been unmercifully brought down time and again on Harold's bared back. He could imagine the pain of it, the hurt and ache which would linger for weeks after such a flogging.

'Yes, they did that in the Legion! They

did that the first time I tried to break away, and got brought back. The bastard of a sergeant major did it to me, while two men held me in the square under the blazing sun. Then they put my tunic on and let it stick to the wounds, and jammed a fifteen pound kit over that and made me do three hours' marching in the sun and sand, until I couldn't pick my feet up any longer. They got two men then and they held me up and forced me to march — until I just went out like a lamp and didn't even know I was marching at all! Then they stripped my clothes off and threw me into a bath of scalding water to cleanse the wounds, and open them up so's any dirt or insects could be washed out. That was only a starter. They'd have done more than that to me if I'd waited for their sentence!'

Jerry compressed his lips and said, 'I'm sorry for you . . . but I expect you deserved it.'

'I don't want your sorrow,' snarled Harold. 'I don't want anything from you except money.' He turned round and picked a bottle up from the corner. He put it to his lips and took a drink of the warm, brackish wine. His outburst seemed to have exhausted him. He said limply: 'Mind picking up my shirt for me, Jerry? It hurts like all hell when I stretch my back to bend.'

Jerry said, 'Not at all.' He stooped, still talking. 'Listen, why not try to change your ways? Go out to South America and make a fresh — *ugh!*'

The bottle hit him with crushing force over the right ear. Then he flopped down on top of the shirt.

Harold stood panting, the bottle held in his hand. His eyes were wild, glazed. His entire body was trembling. He mumbled, 'You pompous swine, you *helped* me to do it! I had it all planned, but you helped me; the way you spoke and acted, it was easy! Oh, *no*, brother — *I'm* not going to South America — but I *am* making a fresh start! I'm going back to *England* — with your passport, and your baggage, and also your money! And not least, *your name too!*

'*I'm* going to be the immaculate, elegant Gerald Mills! *I'm* going to be the

34

one with a reputation for honesty and clean living, and a fiancée, and a business and home! Me! And you — you're going to be *Harold Mills*, deserter and murderer. They're going to find you here, dead. And you're going to have my papers on you, and my uniform by your side . . . and they'll forget all about you and they'll never know that the real Harold Mills is living easy in England — and, if the girl's pretty enough, is happily married! That's why I pumped you, you idiot! And now . . . '

He knelt by the senseless man and started stripping him of his clothing. Then he dressed him in his own shabby blue. Jerry stirred and groaned, and Harold brought down the bottle once more. Then he got water and shaved as well as he could with an old razor the previous occupant had left. He washed his face free of the dirt and grime which was part of the place and combed his hair the way Gerald's was combed. Then he donned his brother's clothing.

There was nothing more to do now but write the note:

'There is nothing for me to live for anymore. The Foreign Legion are seeking me for murder and desertion; I have no money and no friends — I am taking the best way out. H. Mills.'

He laid that note beside his brother's body. Then he went over to the gas tap in the wall and turned it full on. He waited until the smell of gas was almost unbearable, then left quietly, closing the door behind him.

★　★　★

The ship hooted its way out of the harbour at Marseilles. Harold Mills went with it, leaning over the rail and watching the wake receding in the distance. He was thinking, preparing his story for the people he was going back to — the people his brother knew.

For the tenth time he took from his pocket his brother's wallet, opened it, and drew out the photograph inside. It was a photograph of a girl of exceptional beauty, with eyes that were clear and bright, and a mouth that could smile enchantingly. It was signed, 'With love to my darling from Andrea.'

It was his brother's fiancée! And now, Harold meant it to be his fiancée!

He had borrowed his brother's life and clothes. Why not his intended wife?

He went down to his cabin and had another look in the mirror. It was perfect. Not even he himself could have told the difference between Jerry as he had recently seen him, and himself as he was now. The lines on the face were a shade deeper perhaps, and there was something foreign — a cruel expression, not in harmony with Jerry — about the eyes. Yet these were minor things and only noticeable because he was looking for them. But he'd have to change his ways: his manner of speech, his dress, habits, and everything, to carry through the deception.

Fortunately he'd been able to pump all he needed from his now-dead brother. He had the things at his fingertips, the things that Jerry and Andrea did together: riding, swimming, golfing, dancing. He knew about the troubles and successes of the firm, knew just where the chain stores were located.

It wasn't going to be hard — even if they did think him a little strange at first, they wouldn't ever suspect the truth. And when the news that Harold Mills had been found dead in Marseilles came through, they would attribute a great deal of his queerness to that. Yes, it would be simple enough — and he felt, looking again at the photograph, that it was also going to be interesting. *Very!*

4

Return

Barry Arnton paid off the taxi, and he and Andrea stepped into a handy restaurant where they could get a good dinner before the show. Piccadilly was alive and noisy, as usual at that hour of the night. The lights were not yet up, but that didn't detract from the general gaiety.

The restaurant was crowded, but Barry pushed his way through and slid a note into the ever-ready hand of the head waiter. As if by magic he unearthed a table for two in a cosy corner, and they sat down.

The wine waiter came along, and Barry ordered a martini. Then he ordered the dinner, and they sat back to wait. They had to wait for some time, for the place was doing a roaring business, crowded with theatre- and cinema-goers.

Whilst they waited they talked, and Barry grinned. 'Well, Andrea, all being well Jerry ought to be home when we get back from the show.'

She nodded. 'I still think we should have waited in for him. What will he think of me going out the very night he's expected back?'

'He won't mind. And anyway you can tell him I made you. I had the devil of a job to get these tickets — everybody's going to see this play and . . . well, it would have been a shame to waste them.'

'I suppose so. But no late supper after, Barry — we must get straight back. I'm terribly anxious to know how Jerry got on.'

Barry grinned. 'Then it isn't much use my asking you to come back to my apartments and spend the night with me?'

She smiled at him. 'No more use than it was all the other times you asked me.'

Barry said, 'A pity — you ought to see things my way. I'm all for this free love business.'

'Men always are — they don't have to pay!'

'It's a man every time, it's a man,' sang Barry blithely.

Andrea said, 'You're really impossible, Barry. You're hopeless. Whatever made Jerry select you as his friend?'

'Matter of extremes, sweetheart,' Barry told her lightly. 'I'm as big an old roué as he is a prude. That's how we get along. He likes jawing me, and I like shocking him. Works out well.'

She said, 'I don't think you're half as bad as you make out. In fact I'm sure of it — even if I *did go* back to your den of evil that you call your flat, I don't believe you'd know what to do or say. Now be honest — would you?'

'You try me, darling. I've got some colossal etchings, I have really. And you ought to see me in silk pyjamas — '

Andrea said, reprovingly: 'That's enough, Barry. Save your dishonourable exploits for Jerry.'

'All right, if you don't want to hear the fascinating story of my murky past,' chuckled Barry. 'But I warn you you're missing a regular treat.'

Andrea smiled. 'All right. If you're so

keen on having people hear about your amorous exploits, Don Juan, why not write them down and have them published? Then I *might* read them in the privacy of my own bedroom where no one could see my blushes.'

'No good, old girl. No publisher would accept them — they'd be afraid of being sued for publishing pornographic literature.'

'I've no doubt of it,' Andrea murmured.

They had dinner and went in to the play. Considering that the reviews had called it exceptional, they were rather disappointed. The atmosphere in the theatre was stuffy, and halfway through the second act Andrea said, 'Barry, are you enjoying — this?'

'Not a bit, sweetheart. Fact is, for the last ten minutes I've been counting the stray hairs on the head of the bald cove in front of me. Why?'

'Let's go, shall we? It's stuffy, and . . . and anyway I can't help feeling Jerry will be waiting for us.'

'Afraid of him thinking you've been led

astray by his best friend?' grinned Barry.

'Don't fool.'

They left the theatre, to a number of sulphurous glares from the rest of the row whom they had to crush past. Outside Barry said, 'Hold it — there's a pirate!'

'*A pirate?*'

'Mmm. Taxi cab driver with his flag up. *Hoy!*' The taxi cab driver gave him a disdainful glare and swung past.

Barry grunted and stared round. There were plenty of taxis, but all were engaged. He said, 'Now what?'

'Better take the Tube . . . '

'I hate Tubes.'

'Then what do you want to do, Barry? Walk?'

He sighed. 'All right. It's only Uxbridge. We'll take a Tube.'

They went down the escalators with the surging mass of home-goers and caught the Piccadilly Line train. They sat back. It wasn't overcrowded as yet.

Barry suddenly said, 'Well, stew my boots! There's old *Jerry!*' He was looking along the train, directly at a man seated on the end seat, facing them. He got up and walked down the train, Andrea behind him. He sat down beside Jerry, but to his surprise, after one glance, Jerry gave no further sign that he was aware of who had sat beside him.

Barry said, 'Jerry — what's biting you? In a dream?'

The other man looked at him and said, 'I don't seem to — oh, hello!'

'Hello what? Is something wrong, old man? You looked at me as if you didn't know me! Have you got a touch of the sun while you've been in sunny France?'

'Why no — forgive me. I — '

'There *is* something wrong — don't tell me you've only got a 'hello' for the chappie who's been looking after your wife-to-be for the past few days?'

'I — *oh!* Oh, hello. I was thinking — thinking about some personal matters, you know. I'm sorry I seemed so queer.'

'You *did* seem queer — and you haven't said anything to Andrea yet.'

Jerry started abruptly. 'Andrea — but she's — '

He followed Barry's eyes to where Andrea was standing, looking down in surprise. He said, 'I'm sorry, darling. I didn't see you. Miss me?'

She said, 'Jerry — was — was everything all *right?* I mean — you know — did you find him?'

'Eh? Oh, yes, I found him. Yes, everything's fine. Why do you ask? Shouldn't it be?'

'Well of course, dear. But you — you look so worried about something. Your face seems — lined — as if you've been upset.'

He said, 'Nonsense. It's just the strain of travelling, you know. Always leaves me a bit washed out.'

'I hadn't noticed it before, old bean,' said Barry.

Jerry almost snapped, 'Well you've noticed it now, haven't you? Why keep jabbering about it? Forget it.'

Barry said quietly, 'Mislaid your temper over there, Jerry? I'm blessed if I know what you went for, *or* what happened, but it isn't like you to snap at people for being a bit worried about you. What's come over you?'

Jerry made an apologetic gesture. 'It's

nothing. I'm just a bit tired — and worried. You understand. Don't keep on asking me silly questions, Barry.'

Barry said, 'You think they're silly?'

'*Damn* silly!'

The train clattered into Earls Court station. Barry got up. 'I'll leave you two alone,' he said. 'I can get a taxi from here — seems you aren't in a very agreeable temper, Jerry.' He looked at Andrea, who was gazing at Jerry hopelessly. He said, 'Thanks for a pleasant evening, Andrea.' Then he was gone.

Andrea turned to Jerry, who was watching Barry leaving the train with a knitted brow. She said, 'That wasn't very nice of you to act that way with Barry, Jerry. What *has* got into you?'

Jerry shrugged: 'Nothing. Nothing at all.'

'Something must have. Of course, I can understand you being upset about this precious brother of yours, but you shouldn't take it out of your friends. After all, Barry doesn't even know *why* you went to Marseilles.'

Jerry nodded: 'He doesn't, does he? No

. . . but . . . what on earth are *you* doing out with him, if it comes to that?'

She gasped. '*Me?* Have you gone mad, Jerry? You know very well *you* told him to look after me whilst you were away?'

'I did? I mean — of course. I'm sorry — my head's a bit muddled. He has looked after you, then?'

'He's been a darling. Taken me out every night, and always made the inevitable suggestion about me staying the night at his flat.'

Jerry jumped. 'What? Why, the damn *swine* — !'

Andrea almost jumped: 'Jerry what are you *saying?*'

'You say he's made suggestions?'

'Of course. But — we both *knew* he would. You know he doesn't mean anything by them. It's just his way — you're his friend. You know he puts on an act. *Don't* you?'

Jerry passed a hand over his brow and said, 'Why — why of course. I — I get muddled — I'm thinking about — Harold.'

She was sympathetic at once. 'Did everything go all right?'

'I gave him — some money. But — I'm awfully upset about him, Andrea. You see — well, he's had a hard time of it, and he seems to be right in the dumps about everything. He — threatened to take his own life.'

She slipped her arm through his and said, 'Don't worry, darling. You did all you possibly could to help him. Why, after that letter he sent you most men wouldn't have lifted a finger.'

He nodded and said, 'I'll try not to worry, dear.'

She got up and said, 'Well, come on, Jerry. Haven't forgotten your own station, have you?'

He got up and they walked out into the street. She was secretly a bit worried about him. He was acting so strangely. She couldn't help wondering if he'd told her *all* that had happened between him and his brother.

Had she been able to read his mind she'd have had the biggest shock of her life. For he was thinking, *Damn! I've only been with her a few minutes and I've almost given the game away. It isn't as easy as I thought it would be. But Jerry didn't mention leaving Barry to look after her — nor did he mention that Barry was a fool and a clown. I've got to look out or I'll trip myself up! That blasted Barry Arnton looked at me curiously as he left. I think he suspects something's seriously wrong, but of course he can't have any conception of the real truth. Andrea says he didn't know what Jerry had gone to Marseilles for. That's fine, then. No reason why he should be ever told. And that applies to Uncle Jim, too. That shrewd old goat's a dab hand at putting two and two together. Better tell Andrea that . . .*

His thoughts came to an end. He said, 'Andrea, darling . . . '

'Yes, Jerry?'

'I've been thinking — about Jerry — er — I mean Harold.'

'What about him, dear?'

'Nothing — except that I'd rather you didn't mention why I dashed over there. Only you and myself know about it — and, you see, Barry and Uncle Jim might not approve.'

'All right, Jerry. I won't say anything about it. It's your business. To tell you the truth I didn't approve myself, but I knew nothing would alter your mind. Anyhow, you've more than done your duty by him, and he's best forgotten.'

'That's so — he is. Let's not mention him again.' He flagged an empty cab which was returning to town, and they got in. He said, 'Where can I drop you, Andrea?'

'Oh, stop playing the fool, Jerry. I'm staying with you, you know I am.'

He forced a grin. 'Sorry darling. It wasn't really very funny, was it?'

'Not funny at all.'

He cursed to himself. Every slip he made like that was sure to make people more suspicious that something was wrong with him. But as long as they didn't suspect the truth . . .

* * *

Harold got to bed that night without any further mistakes. He was cautious in his movements about the house, feeling his way to make sure he made no prize bloomers. If he'd walked into someone else's bedroom by mistake . . . phew! The thought made him shudder. That *would* take some explaining away.

If Andrea noticed anything else extraordinary, she made no remark, attributing it to his worried condition.

He was late rising the following morning. Andrea was already at breakfast, almost finished in fact. She said, 'Lazybones! You're late.'

'I was tired.' He went round the table and kissed her on the forehead.

She said, 'Mmm. That's the first time you've taken time out to kiss me since you got back, Gerald Mills. Do you know that?'

'I'll make up for it.'

She said, 'You'd better — or I may accept Barry's kind offer and stay at his flat one night!'

He sat down thoughtfully. He was wondering just how far the relationship between himself and Andrea was supposed to have progressed. Was she staying down here as Jerry's *mistress*, until they married? Was that it? Or was she merely spending an entirely innocent visit?

Jerry, of course, had said nothing about anything like that. He naturally wouldn't. But underneath he might be a deep card, the impostor thought. Sometimes these silent ones were . . . and even if he'd never had reason to suspect Jerry of anything like that in the old days, a man can change a great deal in five years.

The girl, for instance. There wasn't anyone at the house but a handful of maids and a cook. No one who might be counted as a chaperone. Now would an innocent girl allow herself to stay at the home of a man who was her intended husband, without a chaperone, from purely *innocent* motives?

He didn't think that possible. He decided he'd have to investigate by degrees. If she was Jerry's mistress and he didn't keep up the alliance she expected, it would make her more suspicious than anything else — and annoyed, too.

He ate his breakfast, then joined her on the terrace. She had on a dressing robe, and it hung open. Beneath the folds he could see the soft roundness of her legs.

She was wearing a scanty two-piece bathing costume.

He said, 'Going bathing?'

She stared at him again. 'We all are! Barry always picks us up on Sunday mornings and runs us to the pool on his property.'

He started. This was the first real stumbling block. He said, 'Not this morning, dear. I — you go with Barry. I can't. I feel off colour . . . '

He knew that if he was forced to don bathing trunks the scars on his back would show accurately enough that he was *not* the real Jerry. The fat would be not only in the fire then, but would be blazing up, too.

It meant he could never go bathing in the company of anyone he was supposed to know again. That in itself would be sure to arouse curiosity. But, he hoped, it wouldn't arouse anything more than that. He could laugh it off by saying he'd got cramp.

Andrea was saying, 'I'll stay home with you, Jerry, if you're feeling ill.'

'No, no, you go ahead and enjoy yourself.'

'But I'd much rather . . . '

'I'll be all right. I'll have another lie down.'

A car horn tootled in the driveway and Barry came up the steps. He looked at Jerry's frowning face and said, 'Hail, smiling morn. Why the awesome frown, Jerry? Not still annoyed about the little rumpus we had last night? I'm sorry I was nasty about it — I realise you must have felt pretty rotten after the trip.'

'No, that's all right, Barry.'

'Then where's the glad rags? The old bathing trunks and whatnot? Not forgotten our weekly dip, have you?'

'No, not at all. Just that I don't feel quite up to it. You and Andrea run along — I'll take a nap.'

'A *nap! You!* My stars, what's come over you? I never did think I'd live to see the day when Jerry Mills would prefer a nap to a dip in the briny. Still, if that's how you feel . . . '

'That's it. I couldn't go in this morning, Barry. Take Andrea along with you.'

'All right,' Barry said joyously. 'Ah, my

pretty wench! Now I have thee in my power! Har, har, har! Pay the mortgage or I foreclose on the old homestead, if I can't have thy favours!' They went off laughing together, leaving the fake Jerry considerably unsettled.

5

The Dream

The dream started that same night.

Harold Mills had settled down a bit into his impersonation of his brother Jerry. The longer he fooled the occupants of the house, the surer he became of himself. And nothing further that day happened to disrupt his mental harmony.

But he was beginning to suffer from the twinges of conscience more than he himself realised. He couldn't drive away the memory of that squalid little room in that filthy building, and Jerry in his white, immaculate suit, stooping to retrieve his unkempt brother's shirt, out of pity for the wounds on that unfortunate's back; and then the bottle descending with skull-crushing impact —

Harold Mills shuddered. It hadn't seemed so bad — *then* —

But now, amongst decent people again,

the full enormity of the crime came to his mind. The more he forgot those terrible years in the Legion, the bigger did his last misdeed become. He had not only killed brutally and swiftly — but he had killed his own twin, the man who had come out especially to help him, and bring him money!

He hated himself for even thinking about it. He hadn't thought he could be squeamish in any way. Perhaps, he thought, it wasn't *his* fault entirely — perhaps there *was* some abnormal bond between twins . . .

He went to bed sorely troubled that night, leaving Barry playing cards with Andrea. He hadn't spoken to them all night — his thoughts had been busy elsewhere. The scars on his back were aching dreadfully, but he was so tired that within ten minutes he was asleep.

He dreamed.

The dream started out on the desert, slogging, slogging through the sand which flowed over his boots; the formed square and the circle of Arab horsemen whirling frantically about it; the dead bodies of comrades on either side. His dream shifted to the fort at Haroun — the battered, blood-stained face of the sergeant major. That dissolved, and in its place was the scornful, contemptuous face of Jerry staring at him . . .

He woke up sweating. Sweat was pouring from him, the bedding was saturated with it, and his heart was thumping painfully. His whole insides were sick, as if they'd been upended and jumbled together. He sat shivering, the clothes thrown from him . . .

And he saw the little man in grey!

He was standing beside the bed, and he wasn't saying anything. He wasn't moving; he was just standing, looking down at Mills. His face was composed, calm, without expression. There was neither accusation nor pity there. His colouring was grey, his hair was grey, and his neat suit was grey, too, He was all grey — the greyness of old and mellowed stones — tombstones!

Harold steadied his hoarse breathing. He whispered, his voice hardly above a croak, 'Who — who are *you?* What do you want?'

The little man in grey didn't move,

didn't speak. He stood as still and straight as a statue, waiting . . .

Mills gathered his courage: 'Go — away!' He thrust out a hand to push the little man in grey from him. The hand went right *through him* — he was a wraith, a tenuous shade of the night, a phantasm of Mills's distraught mind.

And Mills suddenly cringed back, a shrill scream bursting from his lips, for he had seen in the little man's eyes, something which said, *Death*!

He felt he was going to die — his stomach felt churned up.

Then the door burst open suddenly and Barry Arnton, followed by Andrea, rushed in. The lights clicked on.

They found Mills sitting upright, hand to throat, staring at a non-existent something beside the bed. He mumbled, 'He's gone! He's gone — thank God!'

Barry said, 'What *is* the matter, old man? We heard you yell and — '

Mills stammered, 'There was — I was dreaming. And when I — I woke up, he was there — a little man dressed in grey, and — '

'*Then* you woke up?' suggested Barry.

'No — no! I *was* awake already. I was awake when I first saw him — he didn't speak — and when I touched him — God, when I touched him my hand went right *through him*, as if he were a *ghost!*'

Barry murmured, 'Didn't know this place was haunted.'

Andrea said, 'It isn't. You were dreaming, Jerry.'

'No, I tell you! I know when I'm dreaming — d'you think I'm a fool?'

No one answered.

'Jerry,' said Barry, 'are you certain you haven't been — well, mopping it up a bit too Hindi? Honestly, all this sounds to me like a bad attack of the D.T.s.'

'I haven't touched drink tonight. And I can stand my drink anyway. I've never suffered from drunkenness in my life.'

'That's a first-class tall story, old man. It's only a month since Andrea and I had to help you out of Gail Manning's party to keep you from losing your dignity.'

He mumbled, 'Oh — that. I forgot. But I haven't drunk tonight. You both know that. I've been with you two all evening.'

Andrea put her arm about his shoulders sympathetically. She said, 'Don't worry, darling. I know what really *is* troubling you. But you mustn't allow yourself to get upset about it.'

Barry turned away, saying, 'If you two want to be alone . . . '

'It's all right, Barry, you needn't go,' Andrea told him. 'Can I get anything for you, Jerry?'

He nodded; he was recovering himself. 'I'd like something to pick me up a bit — some brandy over there . . . '

'Do you think you ought . . . ?' she said dubiously.

'Damnit, I've told you I'm not drunk. Of course I ought.'

She pursed her lips and poured him a couple of fingers of brandy, which he drank greedily. Then he said, 'Thanks. You can go now. I'm sorry I made such a fool of myself.'

'It isn't like you to have nightmares, dear.'

'It *wasn't* a nightmare. I keep telling you that I was awake!'

Barry chuckled: 'Hell, you aren't going to tell us you really *did* see a *ghost*, are you?'

'I don't know what it was. But it was there! That's all I know!'

They could see he wasn't in any frame of mind to argue. They went out, Andrea kissing him good night tenderly.

Mills turned over and tried to sleep again. But although he left on the light, it was a long time before his whirling mind could drive out the thought of the little grey man who had smelled of the musty odour of long-unopened tombs and damp graveyards!

★   ★   ★

Andrea murmured, 'Barry, I'm worried.'

Barry Arnton nodded. They were standing on the terrace, and he had just announced his intention of leaving when Andrea had come into the open with her thoughts.

'About Jerry, you mean? I can't understand myself. In spite of the fact that he seems too worried to entertain you himself, he also seems to resent *my* being here. I can't make him out . . . he knows that I wouldn't betray his friendship, even if you'd let me, which isn't likely — and yet he looks at me and you as if he suspects we're in something deep together. He's become an outsider to both of us — I mean he doesn't seem to share in the things we all liked anymore. Nor does he confide in us — I'm just wondering how he'll get on at the store tomorrow.'

She nodded slowly. 'He's been queer ever since he came back from Marseilles. I think something must have happened over there.'

Barry said curiously. 'Just *why* did he go?'

'I can't tell you that, Barry. Confidence.'

'I shouldn't have asked. Nevertheless. I don't like it. You saw the way he *kicked* the gardener's dog today — and he was always so fond of old Rover previously. And there was a terrible expression on his face . . . simply because the dog barked at him!'

'That was unusual in itself,' she mused. 'Rover always loved him — never barked at him before for years! Perhaps Rover can sense something strange in his manner . . . '

Barry said, 'You'd better have a chat with him tomorrow and see if you can find out what *is* wrong with him.'

'I will . . . '

'And if you need me for anything — you know my phone number. Good night, Andrea — and try not to worry. Perhaps it's just that he's overworked a bit.'

★   ★   ★

Jerry Mills looked pale and drawn when he came down late to breakfast the following morning. He hardly said a word to Andrea, and what he ate wouldn't have filled a fly.

She broached the subject of his — nightmare — first, after a considerable amount of deliberation. She decided if anything *was* wrong she should know about it.

'Jerry dear, what is wrong? There's something you haven't told me, I'm sure.'

He shrugged impatiently. 'Nothing. I've told you everything.'

'But — that nightmare . . . '

'Forget it. Just a bad dream.'

'You didn't seem to think so last night!'

'I know. It seemed real enough then. Perhaps I'm overworked.'

'Barry said that might be it. You do work far too hard — you don't need to, you know. Old Sims is capable of running the company himself. You could easily retire now.'

'Sims . . . ?'

'Your secretary.'

'Oh, yes. Yes, that's exactly what I'm going to do, darling. I'm phoning up right now and telling Sims that from now on he's appointed general manager at a trebled salary.'

'I think you're wise. But hadn't you better go down yourself to arrange it? There must be one or two little details to settle personally.'

'*No!*' he said sharply. 'No, I've finished bothering myself with the company. It can look after itself. I'm taking it easy from now on.'

She crossed to him and twined her fingers in his hair. 'Jerry, if anything is wrong, why not tell me? You know I only want to help you and look after you.'

He got up impatiently. 'I wish to the devil you'd stop harping on anything being wrong with me,' he said irritably.

He saw she was hurt by his manner and words. He put his arm about her shoulders and said more gently, 'I'm sorry. Just leave me to get over this worry myself, Andrea. I'll be all right in time.'

'All right, Jerry.'

'And — about the wedding, darling — '

'The wedding? What about it, Jerry? It's all fixed up. Aunt Amy's coming down, and my dad and mum. My two sisters are coming as bridesmaids.'

He shook his head. 'I want you to write to them and explain that we'll have to shelve it for a few weeks more.'

'But Jerry — ' she began.

He said, 'Please don't argue the point. I can't marry anyone whilst I'm like — well, like this. Try to understand.'

'I don't understand, Jerry. Why not? Perhaps if we were married you'd feel more settled — and I'd be able to help you more. Besides, I can't go on indefinitely staying here like this, can I? Aunt Amy's *already* passed some very scathing comments about us in her letters.'

'Blast Aunt Amy,' grunted Mills. 'Of course you can stay here, Andrea. I want you here.'

'But not to marry?'

'Don't be ridiculous. Naturally I want to get married — but not for the moment.'

'Then — how long do you plan to postpone the wedding?'

He frowned. 'I can't really say — yet. But trust me, Andrea.'

She sighed. 'All right, Jerry. You know I always *have* trusted you. I'll write Aunt Amy and the others today. Heaven only knows what she'll have to say about it — you know what a suspicious mind she has.'

When he had gone indoors she sat and thought. It was hard to believe he was the same man who had gone to Marseilles the week before. He was far more like the *twin* brother, Harold, she thought. Exactly like the stories he had told her of that brother of his: irritable, moody, easily upset, and rebellious. She did not know how close to the truth she was.

Harold himself had had his reasons for refusing to marry at once. In the first place, he was not yet certain of himself. But the most important reason was that he knew that once married, he could not conceal from his wife the scars on his back. And knowing as she did that Jerry had no scars — she would have seen that when they had been swimming together — she must certainly realise the truth!

Then again, he had no desire to meet Uncle Jim just yet. He knew what a crusty, suspicious old fool Uncle Jim was, and he knew that although the old man's eyesight might not be as good as it had been, his wits were every bit as keen.

No, better to wait a while . . .

Soon he'd take steps to have those scars *removed*.

Unfortunately for Harold, he was destined to meet Uncle Jim that same day. Andrea told him at dinner.

'I telephoned Uncle Jim and told him we'd set the wedding date back.'

'What did he have to say about it?

'He fairly exploded. Said he's coming over right after dinner. Fairly made the earpiece rattle.'

Harold clenched his fingers. 'The damned old idiot.'

'Jerry! He's been good to you — you shouldn't speak of him that way.'

'Why the devil does he have to meddle in my affairs? Why?'

'He's only acting for the best. I suppose he thinks we've had some trifling quarrel and he's coming to put it right. Please don't start any row with him, Jerry. For my sake.'

But it was hard not to start a row with Uncle Jim, when Uncle Jim was on the warpath. Hard for *Harold*. Jerry, with his usual sunny nature, would have laughed it off mildly, and let the old man have his way. Harold was built of nastier stuff.

Uncle Jim blew in like a windjammer under full sail. He came right to the point without wasting any time. 'Damnit young feller, what's this I hear about you putting off the wedding? Hey?'

'It's only temporary,' Harold grunted.
'I don't feel as fit as I should . . . '

'Fiddlesticks! Marriage is just the thing
you want! Liven you up a bit. Serve you
right if Andrea ran off with that Barry
Arnton chap, eh, my dear?' he said to
Andrea.

'Jerry isn't too well, Uncle.'

'Tripe! I'm anxious for you to become
one of the family. If he isn't too well now,
he will be before the date of the wedding.
Simp, that's what you are, Gerald, A simp!
Cancelling the wedding because you've
got a trifling touch of cold or something.
Why, when I was a youth I'd have got
married with pneumonia, if anyone'd've
had me! Pah, you young fellers make me
sick.'

Harold snapped, '*You* don't exactly do
me any *good*, Uncle Jim. There's no sense
in babbling about it. The wedding's off!'

Uncle Jim stared at him and said, 'You
young idiot . . . '

'I said *off*, Uncle! O-F-F — *Off*!'

'Now you listen to *me*, you young
fool — '

'No. You listen to *me*, you old fool — '

'Jerry!' gasped Andrea.

'By George!' exclaimed Uncle Jim. 'So I'm an old fool now, am I? I wouldn't have expected you to say anything like that, Jerry Mills! By George, you sound just like Harold — that scamp of a brother of yours — when he had an argument with me about how he should run the firm. He wouldn't listen to my advice — and see what happened to him! Now you're going the same headstrong way.'

'Look here, Uncle. I don't want to argue and I don't want to hear about Harold. Either stop trying to persuade me you know best, or pick up your hat on your way out! That's all I have to say.'

The old man opened his mouth to speak, his eyes blank with disbelief. Then he tugged at his white moustache, turned on his heel and walked from the room.

Andrea didn't say anything. She went to her room, a bewildered expression on her face. She simply couldn't make Jerry out. The fake Jerry watched the old man into his car, shut the door and walked back. On the hall table was a rolled paper, posted and addressed to him. It was a local paper which he had arranged to have posted on to him from Marseilles. And in a small box it contained a report of the suicide of one *Harold Mills*, in a rooming house near the docks.

6

The Nightmare Again

Harold woke up again with the sweat pouring from him. The nightmare had been horrible enough to wake him up — it concerned scaffolds and nooses and hangmen this time, and always he was the central figure — centre of the crowd, centre of the scaffold, centre of the *noose*.

He lay stiff and sick in the bed, and gradually his eyes grew accustomed to the darkness. Faint moonshine stole in through the far window. The room was quiet and still.

And the little man in grey was there again!

Mills lay perfectly still; he did not scream this time. He held on to his frayed and jangled nerves and lay in the damp pyjamas in the damp bed, his hair hackling on his neck. He stared at the little grey man and muttered, almost inaudibly, 'It's in my *mind* — *all in my mind!* It *must* be — I only have to tell myself it isn't *really* there, and it'll *vanish!*'

He turned his head away. Desperately, he drummed his thoughts into submission. *It isn't there. It's a figment of the imagination; it never has been there! It isn't there — look now, and you'll find it's gone!*

Slowly, carefully, he turned his head. He could tell that if it *was* there, his nerves were going to crack and he was going to have to resort to the emotional safety valve of a scream.

It *wasn't* there! The space beside the bed was perfectly devoid of phantoms, real or imaginative!

He breathed deeply, gathering his control again. He got out of the bed and poured himself some brandy, then got back, turned on the bedlamp, and drew the clothes up to his neck.

Damn silly, he thought. *Little man in grey! Ha! Letting my confounded nerves get the better of me. Must be keyed up very high to think things like that — have to keep control of my mind better than this — dammit. I might imagine anything!* He forced a mirthless grin to his lips, turned to look at the place where the little grey man usually stood to reassure himself — and sank back panting on to the pillow!

He was there again! In the full glare of the electric light!

He looked transparent, and as usual he didn't move or speak. There was something about him that seemed — familiar. Harold knew he'd seen him before — but *where?* And why did the spectre always bring the fear of *death* with him? Why that musty graveyard odour, that stench of rotting corpses?

Mills kept his head; he didn't make any move to get up or to stir. He concentrated on the wraith, telling himself that it wasn't there. He told himself hard, forced himself to believe it wasn't — and it wasn't!

He laughed shakily, turned his head away — and there it was at the *other* side!

That was a bit more than he could stand. What was the good of forcing himself to believe it was nothing but his mind, when the minute he relaxed his thoughts it bobbed up again? He gave a strangled gasp, then a shout of terror. Then he lay quivering in the bed.

The door opened and Andrea came in, her face pale.

'Jerry — what is it?'

'I've — been having a — nightmare again,' he breathed very shakily. 'And I fancied I saw that damned figure — the little man in grey!'

She pulled a chair beside the bed and sat down. She took his hand and held it, and said, 'Darling, you look *terribly* ill. Would you like me to — to stay *here* with you?'

He glanced at her quickly: 'You mean . . . ?'

'I — could sit here, in this chair.'

'Oh, I see . . . '

'Until you fall asleep,' she added.

He didn't want that. When he slept he might dream — and if he dreamed he might *talk* in his sleep — and all kinds of unpleasant facts might come to light. Not only about Jerry, but about the rest of his wretchedly depraved existence.

'No it's all right. I'll be — all right.'

She bent over and kissed him. She was wearing a low-cut gown and the shadowy mystery of the v-shaped hollow below the neckline caused his breath to come faster. He caught hold of her familiarly, but she said nothing. His hand wandered about the smoothness of her dress.

She drew away and said: 'If I can't *do* anything, Jerry — are you sure?'

He nodded. 'Nothing, Andrea. I'll be all right.'

'Try to get some sound sleep, and forget whatever is worrying you so much. Don't fall off thinking about it.'

She went to the door and paused there. The gown she was wearing accentuated the smooth curves of her taut young figure. She said, 'Good night, darling.'

'Er — good night, Andrea.'

When she had gone he lay thinking. He thought of *her*. He had to think of something. He knew that, once he relaxed his willpower, he'd think of that little man in grey again, and the moment he did so he knew the little man would be there — waiting!

The more he thought of Andrea, the faster his blood raced. He already loved her, in the only way he understood love. She was so different to the women with whom he had been forced to consort those past five years. Why shouldn't he take her *now*? She was engaged to him, wasn't she? She didn't seem to mind coming into his room alone late at night. And she had said nothing when he had caressed her a few moments before.

His thoughts ran along lewd lines until the blood pounded frantically through his veins. And unable to think straight, overcome by his passion, he got up, slipped into a dressing gown, and walked from his room.

★　★　★

Andrea undressed slowly, letting each silken garment slip to the floor. She gazed at her white firmness in a mirror, then slid into a diaphanous nightgown.

She was wondering what on earth to do now that Jerry had cancelled the wedding for the time being. Her Aunt Amy — who always had a *great* deal to say in her family circle — would be furious. She hadn't liked the idea of Andrea spending a protracted visit at Jerry's anyway. She knew and liked Jerry — but to Aunt Amy *all* men were alike *inside*, no matter what outer cover they chose to adopt.

Aunt Amy was by way of being bitter. No man had ever attempted to 'get fresh' with Aunt Amy — not because of her formidability, but simply because Aunt Amy wasn't the type you'd *care* to get fresh with. That had jaundiced Aunt Amy badly. She now took the darkest view of man as a sex, and it was her firm conviction that they were all 'up to no good', to put it in her own words.

And Aunt Amy carried *weight*. Aunt Amy was rich, and Andrea's mother and father hoped to cash in on the estate when at length she departed this life for one in which she probably wouldn't be able to interfere as much. It was certain that if Aunt Amy expressed her disapproval, Andrea's parents would do likewise.

At the same time Andrea felt that Jerry needed her there more than ever now. He was ill, that was easily seen. Something terrible was haunting him, making him have those nightmares and act so very differently from his usual self.

But — she couldn't, just couldn't, stay in his home like this, indefinitely. People would be sure to say she was his mistress, and that would just about finish Aunt Amy off.

She had got this far in her meditations when the door opened and Jerry stood there. He looked a little wild about the eyes, she thought, but he spoke rationally enough. 'Not in bed yet, Andrea darling?'

'Why — no, Jerry.' She became aware of his eyes devouring the thin nightdress and she felt uncomfortable. She hadn't ever seen him look that way before — but then, he hadn't ever burst into her room and seen her this way before, either. She reached for a négligé and donned it. She tied the belt and said, 'What is it, Jerry? Is everything all right?'

He fumbled in his pocket and found and lit a cigarette. 'I thought you might care to talk a while. I can't sleep somehow.'

'Why yes, if you can't sleep. Sit down.'

She sat on the side of the bed and nodded to the armchair. He didn't take the hint. He walked across and sat beside her.

'About our marriage — '

'Yes, Jerry?'

'I've been thinking, dear. It may be a few weeks but it won't be longer. No reason why you shouldn't stay, is there?'

'Well, I'll stay until I get objections from my folks.'

'Fine, fine. And . . . ' He broke off.

She waited, and he slipped an arm about her flimsily clad waist. He pulled her closer.

'You *can* see my point of view about the marriage, can't you?'

'I think so. I know how you are at the moment. But — why not try and throw this mental trouble you seem to have off?'

'I am trying — hard.'

'I mean see a specialist . . . a good man . . . Doctor Thorp's noted . . . '

'A doctor can't do anything for mental trouble — '

'Doctor Thorpe's a *psychiatrist!*'

He started. 'You aren't suggesting that — well, that I'm completely *barmy*, are you?'

She smiled. 'Now don't get on your high horse. Lots of people go to Doctor Thorp — many of my friends have been. He can help by finding out just *what* is causing you to be mentally distressed, and he can probably help put it right.'

He grunted. 'Hmmm . . . Let's discuss it tomorrow, Andrea. At the moment it strikes me I've neglected you a great deal since my return; I've been so upset. Why, I doubt if I've kissed you more than about three times . . . '

She said, 'Four, to be exact!'

'Only *four*? Phew! I *must* be losing my mind. Still, there's nothing to prevent me making it up to you now, is there?'

'It isn't very proper, is it?' she murmured slowly.

'Oh, to hell with propriety,' he grunted. 'It's enjoyable and what else counts?'

She stared at him. 'Good heavens, Jerry, you *have* changed! Why, you wouldn't ever come anywhere near my bedroom before you went to Marseilles. Now — '

'Nothing wrong in a few kisses, is there?'

'N-n-n-no, I suppose there isn't. But *only* a few kisses, mind. Then off you go . . .'

He smiled, took her in his arms, leaned down and kissed her. And his kisses were utterly different to the kisses she was used to from him. His lips bore down on hers, moist and devouring. His breath came warm through his nostrils, and he was breathing hard. His arms tightened; his hands . . .

He was pressing the youth and freshness of her to him, thrilling to the warm flesh beneath the thin covering . . .

She broke away suddenly. She got up, and he came after her with arms held out to imprison her again.

'No, Jerry,' she panted. '*Please!* This isn't a bit like you.'

He gripped her by the arm and pulled her hard against him. He husked, 'Andrea — no reason why we shouldn't anticipate the wedding a little, is there? We're *engaged* . . .'

She threw his arm off and tried to keep

the disgust from her face. She said, 'Jerry — I didn't know you were like this! And I had no idea you thought I'd be a willing party to — well, to any suggestions you might make! Please, Jerry — if you don't stop and go to your room I'll *have* to leave *tomorrow!*'

He stood still, hands clenched beside him. He snapped, 'Why, damn it all, what's wrong with you? Frightened of your confounded Aunt Amy?'

'Not at all. It's simply that I don't go in for this kind of thing — not even with a man I'm going to marry. I loathe bedroom farces.'

He sneered. 'I don't know so much . . . the way you talk with Barry Arnton, I shouldn't be surprised if — '

She flushed. 'Don't *dare* say anything, Jerry! You know as well as I do that Barry's only joking — he says it to every girl he meets. Actually he's a lamb, wouldn't hurt a soul. Just likes to think he's bad. He's a *sheep* in *wolf's* clothing.'

He realised he'd gone too far this time. He said, 'Good night, Andrea.'

She said stiffly, 'Good night.'

When he had gone she sat with her head in her hands for a long time. She didn't know what had come over Jerry — but she did know that with each passing day she was feeling less and less affection for him. She hated him for the way he'd been since he'd come back from France. And every action, every word he now spoke, was rapidly destroying the love he'd inspired and built in her before that fateful trip.

Barry Arnton was increasingly more in her mind these days. And she suspected Barry was in love with her — suspected he had been ever since she'd dropped him for Jerry. She was beginning to wonder if she had been wise to do that. There was something very wonderful about dark-haired Barry, despite his banter and chaff.

If he *was* in love with her he'd never mention it, that she knew. He was Jerry's friend — his *finest* friend; they had been at Eton together. It was Barry who had introduced her to Jerry.

Before she finally fell asleep she had decided that it would be best to leave the next morning.

Harold Mills looked more harassed than ever on the following morning; and determined as she had been to leave him, Andrea's loyal nature came to the fore, and she didn't mention her decision, just scrapped it there and then.

He didn't mention the scene in her room at all. She had thought he might apologise, but seemingly he didn't intend to. He said, 'I had a damnable night. Didn't get a wink after I — er — left you.'

She wondered if remorse had caused that. But he soon put her at rest on that question by continuing, 'I was *afraid* to sleep. The fact is, that little man in grey follows me around. Every time I'm not guarding my thoughts he creeps in, and when I look up, he's standing there. Actually standing there.'

She was immediately compassionate. She didn't have to look hard at him to see he was faced with tremendous mental worries. She said, 'Jerry, you *must* see Doctor Thorp!'

'He couldn't help me.'

'He could, I'm sure he could. Why not try him — why not motor up this morning and call on him. He has a place in Harley Street, an office.'

'But wouldn't I need an appointment?'

'He's a friend of mine. If I came along he'd see you right away. Will you, Jerry?'

He thought it over quickly. Perhaps this old fool *could* do him some good, even if it was only a packet of sleeping tablets. No harm in seeing him, and it would set Andrea's mind at rest if he did. He didn't need to tell him *why* the dreams came, just that they did, and that the grey little man was always there. Perhaps the sane light of medical science would ventilate the mustiness of his mind! He said, 'You win. We'll motor up after lunch.'

They did so, with Andrea driving. They were shown into the outer office of Doctor Thorp's consulting rooms by a trim nurse, and the receptionist took their names to him.

He came out almost at once, a fussy old man with sprouting side-whiskers and a bald pate. He balanced gold-rimmed pince-nez neatly on the extremity of a long, thin nose, and he flashed a row of gleaming horse-teeth at Andrea.

'My dear Miss Marsh, how pleasant to see you again. Is this a social call, or have you need of my professional services?'

'Professional services, Doctor Thorp,' she said, smiling. 'It isn't myself — it's my fiancé . . . Mr. Mills.'

Thorp shook hands with him warmly. 'So this is the man you intend to marry, eh? Well, well! And what does he need a man like me for? Eh, young fellow?'

Harold said somewhat surlily, 'That's for *you* to find out!'

The old doctor gave him a keen look, then said, 'Hmm. *No* doctor can make a diagnosis until they know the nature and seat of the pain. The same principle applies to psychiatry, Mr. Mills. You wish to see me immediately?'

Mills nodded.

Thorp said, 'Very well. If you'll wait here, my dear Miss Marsh, I'll take your fiancé into my consulting room and see what the trouble is. You'll find a magazine over there. Will you come with me, please, Mr. Mills?'

7

Nine Months' Wait

The consulting room was furnished tastefully in a modern way, with interior decorating done in light, restful blues. Doctor Thorp indicated a comfortable chair and Mills sat down.

'Now Mr. Mills — I take it Miss Marsh persuaded you to pay me a visit?'

Mills nodded.

'Otherwise you wouldn't have come, eh? You haven't much faith in this sort of thing?'

'I haven't, frankly.'

'That's going to make it rather awkward to begin with — if the patient has faith it naturally helps us a great deal.'

'I don't think you can do anything for me, Doctor. I hoped you might be able to let me have some sleeping pills possibly.'

'If you wanted pills, young man, you could have obtained them from a general practitioner for a consultation fee of five shillings. You may not have faith in psychiatric methods, but at least you should give them a fair trial now you're here. Because this consultation is costing you five guineas anyway!'

He said, 'I will give them a trial. But I still don't see just how psychiatry can help me.'

Doctor Thorp said, 'Let me be the judge of that. Now, name and address, please?'

He gave them; then his age, profession and state of general health. Thorp mused, 'You shouldn't be suffering from any mental afflictions, according to this. A normal man of your age should be perfectly free from repressions and neuroses. However . . . suppose you tell me just what is troubling you?'

So Harold Mills told him of the dreams and the little man in grey, and the fear of death that came to him when the little man was there.

Thorp seized upon the little man at once. 'You say you're quite certain this little man isn't part of your *dreams*, or an aftermath of them?'

'No. He doesn't appear in the dreams themselves at all.'

'And when you force your thoughts into some other channel he vanishes?'

'Invariably.'

Thorp said, 'Is this — spectre, shall we say — anyone you *know*, or have ever *seen*?'

Mills scratched thoughtfully at his chin, then murmured, 'I seem to recollect having seen him *somewhere* before . . . but I really can't say where . . . '

'Think — think hard. Have you seen him, do you think, in the past — say — ten years?'

Mills thought hard and finally grunted, 'I'm pretty sure I haven't, no . . . '

'Before that? Does your memory go any further back?'

Mills shook his head hopelessly. Thorp crossed to the high windows and drew the blue blinds. A restful shade stole over the room. Thorp said, 'Relax in that chair — completely. Don't be worried about anything. Try to think about your childhood. Pick out odd little incidents that have happened to you when you were younger, and do your best to associate them with this little man you claim to have seen.'

Mills tried to make his mind go back. Strangely enough, now that he tried, a flood of memories rushed to him: of him and Jerry at the seashore, taking music lessons, Eton . . . and back further still to the prim little prep school, and the tutor before that . . . There was a gap where he could recall nothing — then slowly came the memory of the night of the car crash which had killed his parents.

Five o'clock by the grandfather clock in the hall — he and Jerry being prepared for bed — and whilst the governess undressed Jerry, himself at the window staring out — and seeing —

The Little Grey Man!

Walking up the path, coming towards the door, as small and as wooden-faced, and as grey and shrivelled as ever!

The maid answering the door — receiving a message from the little grey man, which he, in childish curiosity, had listened to through the keyhole . . .

The message that the car his father had been driving had crashed into a lorry, *killing both his father and mother!*

He said, 'I remember now — where I've seen him before.'

Thorp nodded. 'I'm glad we got it without any further trouble. It was in your childhood, of course?'

'Yes. He was the plain-clothes man who brought the news of the death of my parents in an automobile accident.'

Thorp drew back the curtains again and sat down. He put the tips of his fingers together and looked at Mills. 'That accounts for your impression of death when he appears to you. His bringing the tragic news naturally made an indelible impression upon your subconscious mind at the time. How old would you have been then?'

'I was about five and a half, near as I can guess.'

'A very impressionable age. Things recorded at that time are very seldom forgotten, subconsciously. They linger in the darker part of your brain, and are very seldom tapped. But in times of stress or worry they are apt to crop up again and cause great emotional disturbances in a man. Apparently this little grey man has remained in your head as *the symbol of tragedy and death*. To you he is *death*. And the fact that your imagination conjures him up after all these years tells me that you have great reason to be afraid of your own death in some way. What we have to find out is, what way?'

Mills wondered what he would have said had he known that the fear in his patient's mind was fear of death on the *gallows*!

Thorp continued, 'Something is causing you undue worry — perhaps you know of something yourself?'

'No, I can't say that I do,' muttered Mills. 'I haven't any worries.'

Thorp said, 'We'll try again . . . relax, please . . . ' He shut the curtains and sat at his desk in the gloom once more. He said, 'Just talk . . . '

'Talk? About what?'

'Whatever comes into your mind. We may get something of value. If you don't reveal anything that could be connected with your mental state this time, we'll have to try again later.'

Mills said, 'I still don't understand.'

'I want you to talk. Never mind what you say. Whether it's filth, blasphemy, sedition or treachery. Get it out! I'm a doctor, and anything I learn is confidential, of course. But the basis of psycho-analysis is the mind, and to produce results we must see into the mind of the subjects. Since this is impossible by any method other than direct communication, the subject has to open his or her mind themselves.'

Mills said, 'I see . . . ' He saw that he would have to be very careful indeed. That he would have to keep a close guard on what he said. That he just wouldn't be able to say the first thing that came into his head.

He lay back and thought aloud, 'A country lane in a mist . . . '

Thorp was silent, jotting on a pad.

'A girl beneath tree — a beautiful girl — '

Thorp interposed, 'You'd like to — make her acquaintance?'

'Very much. I haven't the nerve though . . .'

Thorp said, 'Try a fresh angle.'

He thought again, and said, 'The foreign situation — the possibility of war in the future — men being conscripted . . .'

Thorp cut in. 'You're afraid?'

'Not very — no. Just wondering if life *is* worthwhile — what may come in the future — pain, disease, hopelessness, eventually death — and — beyond it?'

Thorp got up. He said, 'Mr. Mills, it's no use. This is a clear example of *controlled* thought! No, don't argue. You're forcing your mind onto those topics! I know. I've psycho-analysed many people — not one in ten think of anything other than their own personal affairs and friends. You're carefully controlling your mind to think of *nothing connected with yourself personally*.'

Mills said, 'Best I can do.'

'I expect it is. Many people involuntarily put up a strong guard, even one they aren't really aware of themselves, when anyone tries to pry into their private affairs.

But in the face of a thing like that I can't assist you in any way.'

Mills muttered, 'I'm sorry . . . those are just the thoughts that came to me . . . '

Thorp drew the curtains back again. 'I know. But they aren't spontaneous . . . you've said it yourself. 'Now what can I think of?' instead of making your mind perfectly blank. And your mind has supplied a topic.'

'Then you can't help me?'

Thorp said; 'Certainly I can. Under hypnosis.'

'Hypnosis? But . . . '

'I'll be able to get behind the screen you've put up that way. That is, if you're a suitable subject for hypnotism. Being, as you are, a sensitive man, I think you will be — if the usual method fails we can try a hypnotic drug . . . '

Mills said, 'No thanks, Doctor Thorp. I don't think I'll put you to that trouble.'

'It isn't trouble. I'll charge you for it.'

Mills shook his head. 'I think there are a few things I'd rather keep to myself, even so.'

'Then you'd prefer to go on suffering

from the nocturnal visitations which your own mind inflicts upon you?'

'I'm afraid so. Perhaps, eventually, they'll wear off.'

'Only by a controlled effort of mind which, frankly, I believe to be beyond your powers.'

'Then I'll just have to stick to the little man in grey, Doctor. Who knows, after a time I may get quite attached to him.'

Thorp shook his head slowly. 'Mr. Mills, from what you've told me it's obvious your mind is in an emotional upheaval — and far from recovering it is likely to get *worse*. Things like this can be brought on by overwork, by the loss of someone precious to you, or by a — twinge of conscience for some wrong done by you — '

Mills snapped, 'What the devil *are* you getting at?'

'I'm merely stating facts. There are a hundred and more reasons for the disturbing condition of mind you are suffering from. You may be on the verge of mental breakdown. If you refuse treatment you are acting foolishly.'

Mills grated, 'I know what I'm doing.

And I see no reason for prolonging this consultation, Doctor. I didn't think that psycho-analysis could help me in any way. I told Andrea so. If you'll be good enough to forward the account . . . ?'

Thorp nodded gravely. 'Very well, Mr. Mills, but if you change your mind at any time, let me know.'

'I won't change my mind, Doctor. Good day.'

He went out, leaving Thorp tapping his teeth thoughtfully with a pencil. Almost to himself he murmured, 'That young man is a fool. I don't know what's worrying him, but he's heading for trouble — even insanity!'

★ ★ ★

They drove towards the West End, and Andrea didn't speak for some time. But finally her curiosity overcame her desire not to intrude on anything he didn't want to tell her voluntarily. She said, 'Well, Jerry? It — isn't serious?'

He said briefly, 'No. Just a matter of strain. It'll pass.'

'Is that what Doctor Thorp told you?'

He said, 'That's what I told Thorp. I knew the man couldn't help me. He couldn't.'

'Did he say so?' she asked anxiously.

'He wanted to put me under hypnotism. I refused.'

'Oh Jerry, why? You want to get rid of — of this trouble, don't you?'

He swung the car viciously between two buses and snapped, 'I'll get rid of it without the help of blasted old charlatans.'

She subsided, hurt. If he refused to believe in the powers of psychiatry, it wouldn't have hurt him to give them a fair try, at any rate; but seemingly Doctor Thorp had said something which had upset him again. Whatever it was he drove on in silence, not even glancing at her.

They came to a halt in the West End, and he set her down in Bond Street. He said, 'I have a business call to make, dear. Will you amuse yourself for a while? Do a bit of shopping . . . or something like that?'

She watched him drive off, after

arranging to pick her up in an hour or so. Then she turned and began to window shop.

Meanwhile, Mills was driving back hurriedly to Harley Street. He hadn't wanted her to know that the 'business' he had was in that particular neighbourhood. He drove along slowly until he found the brass plate he wanted. He got out and walked up the steps.

A trim receptionist admitted him to the hallway. He said: 'Am I in the right place for Sir Arthur Playmer, the plastic surgeon?'

'Yes sir. Have you an appointment?'

'No. But I very much want to see him — could you take my card in?'

She hesitated, then took it from him. She showed him into a cosy lounge and left him there.

She was back inside two minutes. She smiled. 'Sir Arthur will see you now, sir. Will you come with me?'

He followed her along a carpeted hallway to a small door at the far end. She opened it and he walked into the room.

It was an office; the eminent surgeon

was seated behind a desk, busy with some X-rays, but he looked up as Mills entered.

'Mr. Mills?'

Mills nodded, and the surgeon laid aside the plates. He said genially, 'You wished to see me rather urgently?'

'It is urgent in my eyes, Sir Arthur. I should have liked an appointment, but I hadn't decided whom I would go to until I read a report in the *Lancet* of your work.'

'Oh, yes. I recall the paragraph. Won't you sit down?'

He did so and said, 'I understand you have had marked success with grafting over large areas?'

The surgeon nodded.

Mills said, 'Please understand that, as usual, this visit is in strict confidence . . . '

The surgeon raised his eyes and said, 'That is *always* the case, Mr. Mills. Pray go on.'

Mills got up and removed his jacket, then his shirt. He turned to the surgeon and said, 'Can you do anything about — this?' He turned round, exposing the scars on his back.

The surgeon betrayed no surprise. He said, 'I expect I could. You want the scars removing?'

'Entirely.'

'You understand that it would necessitate grafting from your body? The grafts would have to come from other portions of your body.'

'Could you take them from hip and thigh?'

'We could try. Although the logical places would be calf and forearm.'

'That wouldn't do. I — er — do a great deal of swimming,' he said lamely. 'I'd want the grafts taking from a place where the bathing trunks would conceal the resultant scars.'

The surgeon murmured, 'Really, Mr. Mills, that is liable to involve a great deal of pain to you — and a considerable stay in a nursing home.'

'The pain doesn't matter. Can you do it?'

'The expense would be enormous. The scars on your back aren't in a noticeable position . . . you could have a bathing suit with a top, specially constructed to conceal them — far better, from your own point of view, than submitting yourself to nine months of intensive pain, and countless minor operations.'

Mills replaced his shirt. 'Nine months?'

'Within a month or so either way.'

'And can you accept me as a patient immediately?'

The surgeon shook his head. 'I'm afraid not. It would mean your admittance into my own nursing home at Twickenham. At the moment there is not a vacant ward — we have only private wards, you understand, and therefore it would be impossible for us to slip in another bed.'

'What is the earliest date I could expect a bed?' he asked.

The surgeon glanced through a desk file and said, 'About three months, if all goes well.'

Mills nodded. He said, 'I'll take it, Sir Arthur. Now, about a deposit . . . '

8

No Wedding Bells

The angular gentleman turned in at the drive of the Mills residence, gave the place the once-over curiously, then walked right up to the door. He adjusted his flashy tie over his equally flashy shirt front and rang the bell. The maid opened the door to him.

'This is the Mills residence?'

'Yes, sir.'

'Good — *good!* I would like to speak with your master if I may.'

'I'm not sure whether he's in, sir. I'll see — who shall I say is calling?'

He said, 'Merely tell him that my business is urgent. Tell him I think we met in *Marseilles!*'

The girl nodded and left him inside the hall. He inspected the apparent signs of luxury and wealth with a keen eye, chuckling to himself. 'Yes, yes — this bird should be worth a great deal. Say about ten thousand to begin with!'

The maid came back and said, 'Mr. Mills will see you in the library, sir.'

Harold Mills was standing by the mantelpiece, his face a little grey, when the stranger entered. He jerked his hand towards a seat and said, 'Mr. — ?'

'Surely you haven't forgotten our pleasant trip over to Marseilles, Mr. Mills? Remember we spent most of the time together playing cards?'

Harold flushed. 'I'm afraid I have, Mr . . . what is your name, again?'

'Peabody, sir. Mr. *Peabody*. You remember *now*?'

'Of course. Yes, *of course* I remember. How stupid of me. How do you do, Mr. Peabody.'

'I do very nicely sir, thank you. Very nicely indeed. I met some extremely silly people during my stay in Marseilles, of whom you were by no means *the silliest*.'

Harold essayed a nervous smile. He didn't yet know just what his strange visitor was driving at. He said: 'I — er — I'm rather busy at the moment . . . '

'Quite. I have heard that your business is prospering?'

'You have *heard?*' queried Harold, cautiously.

'To be more truthful I might say that I made it my special mission in life to — er — *find out*. What I have found out has convinced me that you are a very prosperous man, Mr. Mills, while I — *I* have to eke out a miserable and unenjoyable livelihood by card sharping and similar little games. You might call me an adventurer — although on the boat, I recall, when you found that you were losing an incredible amount of money to me, you taxed me openly with sharp practice! Remember?'

Mills mumbled: 'I have no idea why you have paid me this visit — nor can I approve of your apparently insolent enquiries into my affairs . . . '

'No? Then I should perhaps make myself a little clearer. You remember that you were worried on the voyage, and you had, furthermore, been taking rather unwisely to drink, which it was plain you were unused to. I, my dear sir, was your drinking companion. It was not until later that we had our trifling tiff concerning marked cards — and during that tiff, when I applied an opprobrious expression to you, you attempted to strike me . . . you recall that incident?'

'I — I do,' lied Harold.

'Hmmm. You slipped and fell — and your wallet fell from your pocket! I picked it up — and I found inside, in addition to the notes it contained, *a letter!* I returned the notes, but retained the letter, and before you could have had time to discover its loss, the boat had docked.'

'A — a letter?' gasped Mills. '*What* letter?'

'A letter with which, in the near future, I hoped to force you to make a contribution towards my own income. A substantial contribution. *A letter which was clear evidence that you meant to break the law by that trip to France, and assist your worthless brother to escape recapture.*'

Mills sat down abruptly. He said, 'Well?'

Peabody lit a thin cigar and blew smoke at an ornamental jar on the sideboard.

'That letter, of course, made it clear to me that you were going to help your twin brother who was, apparently, in distress of some kind. I decided to keep an eye on you . . . and did so. I marked your visit to the house at which your brother was staying, and I noted that you were there some time, presumably giving him not only the money you brought, but also a lecture. Then I saw you return to the landing stage . . . '

'And then . . . ?'

'The following day I read the report of how your brother had committed suicide by leaving the gas tap turned on!'

Mills got up. He snapped, 'And what is all this leading up to? Since my brother is now dead it doesn't matter what you do with the note. If, on the strength of that, you expect me to give you *money* — '

'Not on the strength alone of what I have told you, Mr. Mills. There is *more* yet: I made it my business to find out the *details* in the case of your brother's suicide. Having some slight interest in the affair, this was natural. And what do you think I *found?*'

109

Mills clenched his fists tightly. Peabody continued: 'I found, Mr. Mills, that the police were considerably puzzled by your brother's corpse!'

'In — in what way?'

'It appeared that the Legion claimed the man they wanted had a badly scarred back from a recent flogging. The man found by the police proved to be *devoid of scars* of any shape or size! And, in addition to that, he seemed to have been *struck on the head* prior to his death! Now the police are easy in Marseilles, and they glossed the matter over. After all, the servant Roella had sworn that Mr. Mills had had *no visitors* since his arrival there, so why *should* they suspect foul play? They assumed, with regard to the scars that had vanished, that the Legion had been *mistaken* in saying the man had been flogged recently. How, they wanted to know, *could* there have been foul play? Legion officers had testified that the dead man was indeed *Harold Mills!* They knew nothing of his personal history, and it was, indeed, untraceable. So the matter drifted from one to the other, and gradually became forgotten with the burial of the body. Unfortunately from *your* point of view, I did *not* forget it! That is why I am here — Mr. *Harold Mills*!'

'*You fool*,' panted Mills. 'Get out before I throw you out! You don't expect me to listen to this fantastic fable, do you?'

Peabody shrugged. 'As you wish. No doubt the police in Marseilles would listen to it. They would, I expect, be very enlightened to learn that M'sieur Harold Mills had a *twin* brother who paid him a visit before his death — just a matter of minutes before!'

Mills gasped. 'But in the face of the evidence of the girl, Roella, that Mills had *no* visitors . . . ?'

'That was the story she gave to the police. I had a little chat with the girl, Mr. Mills. She — er — seemed to know you rather *intimately*, hmmm? She vouched that you *had* had scars upon your back — she also informed me that you had given her fifty francs to testify as she did! It cost me one hundred francs to secure the information I desired — but I have in my possession a signed statement from the girl — stating she gave *false* testimony.'

Mills snarled, 'She wouldn't be fool enough to sign a thing like that . . . '

'Wouldn't she? She was a rather ignorant girl — very badly brought up, I fear. So different to you and I. She didn't quite realise the consequences of deliberately perjuring herself to aid a murderer! She was only too anxious to get her fingers wrapped around the money I offered her. So, Mr. Mills, I have the confession — and you have your brother's name and money — and freedom! Now what could be more agreeable than that you should exchange some of the money for my little document?'

'You know the penalty for blackmail?' snarled Mills, his face white with rage.

'Indeed I do. Hardly so severe as the penalty for — *murder!*'

Mills hissed, 'What do you want?'

Peabody smiled and spread his hands. 'A trifle. You won't miss it, since it isn't your money anyway. Shall we say, to begin with — ten thousand pounds?'

Mills panted, 'You're insane. Where could I get ten thousand from?'

'I have already told you I have been secretly making enquiries as to your financial position. I find that you must have accumulated a considerable sum — about fifty thousand, and more coming in every day. I *should* say that your *brother* must have accumulated that amount, really. But since it is now yours we won't mince matters. What do you say? Ten thousand for the paper — or the hangman's noose for you, if not the guillotine!'

Mills took a pace up and down the room. Then he faced the blackmailer and said savagely, 'What guarantee have I that you'll let me alone after that?'

'None, Mr. Mills. In fact, I shall probably bleed you white. The confession is immaterial — but the scars on your back will always be sufficient proof for the inquisitive. However, you'll just have to do as I ask — otherwise I can see nothing but ill fortune in store for you!'

Mills grated, 'You — !'

Peabody smiled. 'I am very well

attuned to insults, Mr. Mills. At the same time I object to words like the one you just employed. Allow me to inform you that my father and mother were respectable people, respectably married by a responsible minister of the Church. The remark you have now uttered is slanderous in the extreme — therefore I have no alternative but to raise the cost of the first payment to — say — twelve thousand pounds?'

Mills sank down into a chair. After a moment he looked up at the blackmailer. 'And — what do you think my friends, fiancée, my bankers will think if I draw such an amount in currency?'

'That shall be your concern. It will be nothing to what they would think if you were dangled by the neck from some rough scaffold one fine morning. Now, Mr. Mills . . . ? What have you to say?'

Mills got up and nodded. 'What can I say? You have the whip and you are cracking it. I'll pay you.'

'Excellent. I probably won't make any further demand on you for at least a year. I should be able to manage admirably for that length of time on twelve thousand, expensive as are my tastes.'

Mills told him, 'I'll make the payment tomorrow. I'll visit my bank first thing in the morning — but don't come here again.'

'As you wish. Where, then, can we meet?'

'There's a spinney at the far end of Morton Lane — about fifteen minutes' walk from here. I'll meet you there — and don't forget the confession! If you don't bring that the deal's off!'

'Have no fear, Mr. Mills. But if you consider that with the confession in your possession everything is all right, you are very much mistaken. I will be at the agreed spot at, say six — '

'Not that early. I may not have returned from town. Make it nine o'clock.'

'If you wish. Good night, Mr. Mills. No, don't trouble. I can find my own way out.'

The door closed behind him and Mills, with a face pale and lined, sank down into a chair. He knew what he was in for — an unscrupulous bleeding, by a monster of iniquity almost as ruthless as was he himself. Nor could he appeal to the police in this case. The money would be easy enough — he could spend time in copying his brother's signature onto a cheque — but Peabody had as good as hinted it was not to end there!

He started up as the door opened and Barry and Andrea walked in. Barry said pleasantly, 'Who was the human vulture who just left?'

'A — a business acquaintance of mine. Man I know. Just came to see me about a — a financial matter. Not important.'

'It looks important,' said Barry, puzzled. 'You look as white as a freshly laundered sheet. It isn't that you're in any money difficulties, is it, Jerry? Because if so, I'll — '

'No, it isn't that. I'll be all right.' He pulled himself together with an effort. 'Been dancing?'

'Riding — getting a bit too dark now. Thought you were coming with us tonight?'

Harold looked apologetic. 'I didn't feel in the mood. You know how I've been lately.'

Barry said suddenly, 'What's this fearful bilge about the wedding being postponed? Andrea was telling me. You mean to say you aren't going to tie the happy knot after all, this weekend?'

'I'm afraid not. Have to put if off for a bit longer.'

'But why? After I've been to all the trouble of getting my morning suit out of the mothballs, and evacuating the moths to my Eton blazer! As best man I don't mind telling you I'd been looking forward to a spot of froth and frolic with the bridesmaids. Now you intend to deprive me of the opportunity of showing them my etchings!'

Andrea said, 'I can understand Jerry's point of view. But it won't be for long, will it, Jerry?'

He fumbled with his tie and said, 'Well really, Andrea — the fact is, I'm afraid it'll be a bit longer than I thought. I — I have to make a business trip in about three months' time — and I expect to be away for *nine months*. I don't want to get married until I return — so I'm afraid it'll be almost a year, my dear.'

Andrea gasped. 'A — a *year*? *Oh, Jerry*, but you *said* . . . '

'I know, I know. I'm sorry, but that's how it is. This trip is urgent.'

Barry grinned. 'You want to watch out — by the time you get back you may find your best man's persuaded the bride to see his etchings! But I've an idea — why not get hitched, *then* take the little woman on this trip *with* you? Eh? Make it a sort of business-cum-pleasure trip — '

Mills shook his head stubbornly. 'I don't intend to marry before I go. Besides, it isn't the kind of trip that would be suitable for a young girl.'

Barry said, 'Hello, you old dog! Where *are* you going?'

'I can't say. But I couldn't take Andrea. Impossible.'

'I'll bet you're having a final fling,' grinned Barry. 'And what a fling you must be planning! Nine months, eh? Whew!'

Mills snapped, 'There's nothing like that about it. It's a business trip, plain and simple. Now don't keep going on about it.'

Andrea spoke for the first time for

some minutes. She seemed to have had a severe shock. She said, 'Of course, Jerry, you know this will make it impossible for me to stay here any longer?'

'Why will it?'

'Why — well, Aunt Amy . . . '

Harold snarled, 'Who's in love with me? You or Aunt Amy?'

Andrea murmured quietly, 'I'm not so sure now, Jerry.'

'What do you mean by that?'

She opened her mouth, then shut it again. Without another word she walked to the French windows, opened them, and went out.

Barry wrinkled his brow and stared at Jerry. He said quietly, 'I must say, you're behaving rather queerly, old man. It isn't like you to treat Andrea that way.'

Mills scowled. 'She should try to understand then. I can't help it if I have things that must be done before I marry . . . more important things!'

Barry grunted, 'I didn't think I was exactly old-fashioned, but you beat even me! I do consider marriage to be a pretty big step — seemingly you don't think it's a matter of importance at all.' He turned on his heel and followed Andrea onto the terrace.

★ ★ ★

They went to a dance the following night — without Jerry, who had elected to stay at home again. But halfway through, Andrea said she felt sick through the closeness of the atmosphere, and they came home to the Mills place. Jerry wasn't about, and they sat in the library talking. Jerry came in about ten minutes later, at nine fifteen. He came in hurriedly through the French windows and started wiping dirt and grass from his shoes before he noticed them. He was hatless and coatless.

Barry called, 'So *there* you are! The maid said you were in the library — said you'd told her you *weren't going out!* Where've you been?'

Mills snapped upright. On his face was a terrible look of rage. He grated, 'Damn you, are you *spying* on me?'

9

Murder!

They stared at him in blank amazement. His face was livid with fury, his hands knotted by his sides, his breath coming hard through clenched teeth. He repeated harshly, 'You've been *spying* on me — '

Barry got up. 'Don't be a damned fool, Jerry. No one's been spying on you! What is there to spy on?'

Mills came towards him his face working. He snarled, 'You were supposed to be at a dance with Andrea! What brought you home so early?'

'It was hot and unpleasant. Andrea felt ill.'

'That's a damned *lie!*' he shouted thickly. 'You came back to see what I was doing — why I wouldn't come with you! Perhaps you think I'm up to something . . . '

Barry grunted, 'Far as I can see there

isn't anything you *could* be up to — at the same time I'll be getting suspicious, the way you're carrying on!'

Mills calmed down suddenly — too suddenly to lull suspicion. He flopped into a chair and said, 'I — I've been out in the garden for a walk. That's all. Just a breath of air . . . '

'Who said you hadn't? And what does it matter anyhow?'

'It — it doesn't. I'm afraid I let my temper get out of hand. Barry — Andrea — I — er — apologise.'

Barry said, 'Accepted. But aren't you letting your temper get out of hand, as you call it, rather too much lately?'

Mills looked at him evilly and said: 'If you don't like it you don't *have* to put up with it, Barry. You have a home of your *own.*'

Andrea gasped. '*Jerry!* Barry, don't take any notice. He's ill.'

Mills continued, 'I know what I'm saying quite well. There's the door, Barry. If you feel I'm getting a bit too much for you to put up with, you can go.'

Barry picked up his hat from the table

and said, 'All right, old man. I never was the kind of character that needed telling twice. Night — night, Andrea.'

She said quickly, 'I'll come to the door with you.'

They walked into the hall, leaving Mills sitting slumped in his chair. At the porch, Andrea turned to Barry and murmured, 'Barry, don't take any notice of — of Jerry. I'm sure he isn't in his right mind, quite, at the moment. He'll be sorry for what he said tomorrow.'

'Then he'll be able to make an apology.'

'Don't be like that, Barry. Remember how long you've known him, ever since Eton . . . he's been as good a friend to you as you've been to him . . . he wouldn't desert you if *you* were in trouble.'

He wavered. 'Well . . . '

'And — *I* need your help, too. I wouldn't know what to do if you weren't here every evening. Honestly, Barry, I'd go mad.'

Barry looked at her. She seemed so young and sweet and helpless standing there with her face upturned. He fought a strong desire to take her in his arms and kiss away her troubles. But instead he said, a little unsteadily: 'Why don't you go away until Jerry's back to normal?'

'I want to. But don't you see, Barry, if I did that just because he's ill, what would people think of me? What would I think of myself? I loved him enough when he was fit and well and cheerful — I was happier than I could have said. You wouldn't think much of me yourself, in spite of your advice, if I ran out on him now, when he most needs me, would you?'

'That's the point — *does* he need you? Does he need *me?* He seems to be pretty self-sufficient, ill or not.'

'Let's not argue. He may *think* he doesn't need help, but he does. We both realise that. And — as his fiancée and his best friend, it's our duty . . . '

Barry grinned infectiously and stuck out his hand. She caught it as he said, 'You win. We'll stick by him, you and I. If there's anything we can do at all, we'll do it.'

Impulsively she reached upwards and

kissed him lightly on the lips. For some minutes he just looked at her strangely. Then he seemed to come to himself again. He laughed, 'Better not make that a habit, Andrea, or you'll have me renewing my invitation to come and see my etchings! Good night.'

She watched him striding away in the misty night under the dark shadows of the trees, and a wave of nostalgia swept over her. There was a wistful expression in her eyes. She shrugged and turned back to the house.

Mills was still slumped in the chair in the library. She said, 'Hadn't you better go to bed, dear?'

He looked up at her. 'I expect you think I've behaved rather boorishly?'

'I think you were downright rude,' she said, drawn by his sneering expression. 'It's a wonder Barry puts up with you at all. You've changed entirely.'

'I can very well do without *Barry*,' he grunted. 'And for that matter I can do equally as well without *you*!'

She almost reeled. It was so unexpected. She said faintly, 'Is — is this what you've been leading up to?'

'How do you mean?'

'The way you've been acting — tonight, for example, when you came in through the windows . . . '

'You gave me a shock then. I'd expected to find the library empty. It wasn't. Wouldn't it have given you a shock? No, it's just that — want me to be blunt?'

'Please do!'

'Very well. It's just that I'm about *fed up with both you and Barry. I* can get along quite easily without you — I've made up my mind to that.'

'You mean — the marriage is off *altogether?*' she asked, feeling suddenly cold inside.

'That's *just* what I mean. So if you can make arrangements to leave tomorrow . . . '

She said quietly, 'I'll leave *tonight.*'

'There's no need to do that.'

'You don't think so? I do.'

She turned and walked from the room. He sat on for a time longer. He was wondering if she'd think it was too sudden. He wanted her, but not in the same way that his brother had wanted

126

her. It meant undergoing the grafting — and his nerves were so shot now he decided he could not stand up to the pain that was sure to entail, nor to the enforced inactivity. No, she would have to go — the wedding would have to be cancelled. But — would it make people suspicious?

He got to his feet and went up to her room. He opened the door without ceremony. She was in her underthings, and she grasped a dressing robe and put it on hastily as he entered. She said, 'Isn't it customary to knock at a girl's door before you come in?'

'Don't act the goat . . . '

'I'm not acting the goat! You and I are nothing more than acquaintances now. You haven't the right to take any liberties.'

'I came to see if you knew how it was . . . I mean why I've cancelled the marriage.'

'I think I can guess. The other night you came to my room to — 'Her voice became scornful. 'To indulge yourself in my favours. Seemingly you fancied I'd be only too willing to accommodate you, Jerry. When you found out your mistake you were mad. And now — well, it looks as though that was all you wanted from me. If it was, you're unlucky. But don't be upset — there are plenty of girls who'd be willing to share an affair with a man who's as wealthy as you are.'

'It isn't that at all. It's just that I don't think I have the right to marry any girl at the moment. You know how I am with this mental trouble.'

'It isn't *that* — you've *cancelled* the wedding now, not merely *postponed it*.'

He fumbled with his cigarette case and lit one. He said, 'How are you going to get home?'

'There's a train leaving at ten thirty. You can have my luggage sent on.'

'I'll drive you to the station . . . '

'Don't bother.'

He grunted and watched her packing silken things into her case. He said, 'After all, you've still got Barry . . . ' with a sneer in his voice.

She replied quietly, 'Yes, I've still got Barry.' She locked the case, then looked at him. 'Would you mind making yourself scarce whilst I change?'

He turned and walked out. Then he inserted his head again.

'You needn't bother to slip in on me to say good-bye. I'm going to bed.'

'I had no intention of doing so.'

The door closed behind him, and with compressed lips she went on with her packing

Mills went to his room, uncorked the brandy bottle and took a long pull without bothering to use a glass. The brandy glucked in the bottle, and when he put it down fully two inches had gone. He lay on the bed coughing, with all the lights full on.

He got up when the coughing bout was over, extracted two slips of paper from his pocket, and read them. One was the letter he had written to Jerry from Marseilles. The other was a document signed by Roella in a very bad scrawl, testifying that she had given false witness, and that M'sieu Mills had been visited shortly before his death by a man who looked exactly like him — and that M'sieu Mills had later bribed her to say nothing of this fact.

He screwed them into balls, struck a match, and touched it to them. He watched them burn to ashes in the ash tray, then crumpled the ashes in his hands.

He took another drink from the brandy bottle and lay fully clothed on the bed. Sleep refused to come. He closed his eyes and tried to make his mind blank, but failed. Thoughts — sinful, whirling thoughts, raced through his conscious mind. In his memory he relived his murderous deeds over and over.

Then the little man in grey came again.

Mills lay staring at him, trying to make him go. But now, no matter how hard he tried, the vision remained. The same inscrutable, wooden face; the same neat grey suit; the same greyish-coloured hands and staring grey eyes.

Mills tossed and turned and groaned. He got up and left his bedroom and went down into the library. He sat in the easy chair with the brandy bottle in his hand.

The little grey man was there again, in

front of him this time.

'You fool,' he told himself. 'Forget it! It's imagination; that damned psychiatrist told you that. Forget it and it'll go. It's nothing — only something conjured up out of the black recesses of your subconscious. It can't *harm* you!'

He tried to persuade himself, but it was useless. The little grey man still stood there — waiting. And the smell of death and decay became stronger, and despite the fact he knew it sprang from his mind alone, it was real enough to him.

He stood up and shrieked at the little man, 'Get out!'

The little man remained. Mills screamed again, 'Get out, get out, blast you! Get *out!*' and in a frenzy he threw the brandy bottle at him. It went right through the wraith and shattered against the far wall.

Andrea, passing the library door with case in hand, heard the shriek and crash, and paused.

Was she being fair to leave him alone in his condition? He had thrown her out, certainly, but he wasn't responsible for what he did, that was positive.

And yet — how could she stay?

Tentatively, she opened the door and peered in. Mills was slumped across both arms of the chair, his head hanging. For a moment she thought he was dead. But then he groaned, and hanging there like that, began to sob . . .

Silently she closed the door again.

She went outside and turned down the drive. She walked along the road to the station and took her ticket. She had a wait of ten minutes, and she employed them by opening her case and taking out a letter-card on which she wrote:

Dear Barry,

I'm very worried about Jerry. I'm going home — and I hate to leave him like he is now. He's worse than he's ever been before. Far worse. Don't let him send you away, too, Barry. Try to help him — not for what he is now, but for what he *has* been to both of us. If you want to see me I'll be staying with Aunt Amy for a while.

Don't let poor Jerry down.

My love,

Andrea.

She addressed, sealed and posted it,

then caught the train to Aunt Amy's. She knew Barry would do all in his power to help his friend. He was built of that kind of stuff, and in face of her appeal he'd try his hardest to drag Jerry up from the black pit he seemed to be in.

That was all she could do . . . leave it to Barry.

Her confused thoughts blending with the whirring of the wheels on the track, she dozed.

★   ★   ★

The headlines of the late-morning *Daily Bugle* read:

MURDER MYSTERY AT TWICKENHAM!
UNKNOWN MAN FOUND STABBED TO
DEATH IN LONELY SPINNEY!
POLICE BAFFLED!

'Late last night a tall, thin, middle-aged man dressed in dark, somewhat threadbare clothing, was found in an old Spinney at Twickenham. He had been stabbed viciously five or six times in the back, and one of the thrusts had penetrated the heart. Police surgeons give it as their opinion that this man was stabbed at about eight to ten o'clock last night. The wounds indicate that the man was standing waiting for someone at the time, and that the killer crept up on him and struck without warning, whilst the murdered man's back was turned.

'No marks of identification were to be found on the body, and a description of the man, together with a photograph, is appended below.

'The body was discovered by a tramp who had chosen the spinney as a resting place for the night, and whom the police are holding for further questioning.

'Investigations are proceeding in the capable hands of Inspector McGuire of New Scotland Yard.'

Barry laid down the paper and made a thoughtful crack in the shell of his weekly ration of egg. He looked at the photograph of the dead man again; in the usual way of news photos it was blurred and indistinct. And yet there was a familiarity about it. Somewhere he had seen that man before — and unless he was much mistaken it was the same person he had seen leaving Jerry's home only two nights previously!

Of course he hadn't had a good view of the man — but there couldn't be very many people in those parts with that peculiarly aquiline cast of countenance, surely?

If it were the man — what did that signify?

His meditations were brought to an end by the entry of his valet, Percival, bearing a letter-card.

'Eleven o'clock post, sir.'

'Thanks, Percy. Late as that is it?'

'It *always* is, sir,' said Percival meaningfully, and Barry smiled and said, 'I'll have to start rising earlier, Perce. Things are happening while the young master lies abed, what? Juicy murders and all that.'

Percival nodded. 'We have read about the spinney murder, sir?'

'We have — just. What are your own views?'

'We are of the opinion that the tramp did it, sir.'

'Hmmm.' Barry thumbed open the

letter-card and the excellent Percival withdrew noiselessly.

The card was from Andrea, telling him she was leaving, and asking him to look after Jerry.

He murmured to himself, 'I think Jerry *needs* some looking after at that. It was about nine that he must have been out of the house last night, after telling the maid he was staying in. And the grass and dirt on his shoes — ! And then his fright when he realised someone had seen him sneaking into the jolly old ancestral home again! Now exactly *what* has old Jerry been up to?'

He looked at the photograph again and grunted, 'Not that the chap didn't look as if he deserved to be murdered. But one can't have one's friends hopping about doing things like that. I'd better make an effort to go over and see Jerry Mills!' He rose lazily and made for the bathroom.

10

Soho Lady

Mills was sitting in the morning room, toying with a plate of kidneys and bacon, when Barry walked in. He looked up, and seeing who his caller was, said, 'I thought I'd seen the *last* of you?'

Barry held his temper with an effort. He sat down in the chair opposite Mills and faced him across the table. 'Sorry to disappoint you, old man, but one doesn't get rid of one's friends *that* easily. I'm not going to let that silly squabble of the previous night make any difference to us.'

'I am.'

Barry bit his lip.

Mills went on, 'If you're looking for someone to show your etchings to, Andrea went home last night.' His voice was a drawling sneer, and Barry felt himself getting red under the collar.

He took the folded paper from his

pocket. 'I suppose you've heard?'

'Heard what?'

'About the — murder. In the papers this morning.'

Mills raised his brows enquiringly. 'What's so special about this murder? There's generally one every morning. Why should I concern myself about this one in particular?'

'Simply because it happened quite near here!'

'Really? What am I supposed to do now? Go into hysterics and call for police protection?'

Barry threw over the paper. He said, 'Look at the photograph — friend of yours, isn't he?'

Mills hardly glanced down. He lifted his coffee cup and took a sip. He said, 'Too sweet.'

'I asked you about the man in that photograph. You know him, I think — and the police don't. Therefore it's up to you to put them right.'

Mills picked the paper up. He grunted, 'I never saw him before in my whole life.'

'What?' Barry came to his feet, mouth

open. He gasped, 'Are you trying to say that that isn't the — business acquaintance who visited you a couple of nights ago?'

'I most certainly am. Nothing like him.'

Barry snapped, 'It looks like him to my eyes.'

'Then you need your eyesight seeing to, I'm afraid. Just *how* closely did you see this man?'

'Not very close — but close enough to have a pretty fair idea that he was something like the murdered man there!'

'Only a *pretty fair* idea, eh?'

Barry said, 'You were out last night between the hours of eight and ten, weren't you?'

'Was I?'

'You know you were. And we saw you.'

'What has that to do with anything?'

'That man *was murdered between those hours!* Does *that* spell anything to you?'

'Yes — it spells that someone must have had it in for him. Any more questions?'

Barry stared him in the eyes. '*You*

couldn't be that someone, could you?'

'I *could* be — but I'm *not*.'

'Are you sure?'

Mills yawned visibly. He said, 'My dear man, even if I were I wouldn't *tell* you. You seem to be pretty sure *yourself*. Then why not go ahead and *prove* something? Why annoy *me*?'

Barry said, 'Listen Jerry, be yourself. For God's sake be yourself! I can see that this cool and collected act of yours *is* an act! I'm not blind — underneath you're as jittery as hell. Look at the way your hand wobbles when you raise your cup.'

Mills began to get angry. 'Mind your own business, Barry, can't you?'

'I'm only trying to help you, that's all.'

'I've already declined your offer of help — without thanks. I can do all the helping I need myself!'

'You'll help yourself right into a noose!'

Mills snarled, 'You seem to be very certain that *I* killed the fool! You're as good as calling me a *murderer!* Yet you say you want to *help*?'

'I am certain you know *something* about it. And I'm telling you that if you *didn't* have any hand in the murder, you ought to put the police right as to his identity.'

'I've told you I don't know him. Haven't seen him before in my life. If you think differently go and repeat your story to the police — see what they make of it! They can question me but I can't tell them any more than I've told you — because I don't *know* any more!'

Barry said, 'I wouldn't go to the police. And you know I wouldn't. But I do think . . . '

'That's the trouble. You think too much. Let the police do their own thinking. See how far they get without your help, or mine either.'

Barry grunted, 'Listen to me, Jerry. Every word you say, every move you make, makes you look guiltier in my eyes. But if you *did* kill him I'm pretty sure you had a good cause. You're in some kind of a jam — I don't know what, but whatever it is it's changed you from the man we knew and admired into a surly, hot-headed, addle-brained neurotic! Now why not spit it out? Why not let the people who're willing to stand by you give you a hand? Tell *me* — tell me what's wrong, and I'll do everything in my power to help you out!'

'You can't help me out of anything,' he retorted. 'Simply because I'm not *in* anything! And you're wasting your time anyway.'

Barry got up and took his paper. He said, 'Very well, Jerry. I'll leave it to you — would you rather I went along to the police with this paper and told them what I know — or would you rather I didn't? Which?'

'If you put it *that* way I'd rather you *didn't*.'

'Then just make a clean breast of it to me.'

Mills got up, holding his serviette tightly between his fingers and thumbs. He walked across and shut the door. Then he turned back to Barry and said: 'You're poking your nose into a very risky business.'

'That doesn't matter.'

'Not now — but you're liable to come to grief.'

'I'll chance it. You *do* know this man, don't you?'

Mills said, thinking fast, 'I know him.'

'*Then* — ?' Barry went on.

'His name is — rather *was* — Mister Peabody.'

Barry lowered his voice. 'And you — killed him?'

'No! I did not kill him — but I would have done so if someone hadn't beaten me to it.'

'I don't believe that, Jerry.'

Mills came over and looked down at him. He said softly, 'Listen, Barry, since you've more or less got me in a cleft stick anyway, I'll play the game with you. I admit it'd make things awkward for me if you were to tell the police what you know. So provided you agree to say nothing . . . '

'I do agree. The last thing on earth I'd want to do would be to give you away.'

'*I did kill him, then.* Now you know! I sneaked up on him through the shrubbery after fixing an appointment, and I stabbed him with an old knife, which I later threw into the river!'

'But — but *why?* What made you do such a thing?'

'That's easy — he wasn't fit to live any longer. He was a blackmailer!'

'*Blackmail?*'

'Exactly. He was forcing a payment of twelve thousand pounds from me — otherwise he was going to tell something to the police.'

Barry clenched his fists until his knuckles whitened. 'He was going to tell — *what* to the police?'

'About something I did — against the law. I suppose you could call it aiding an escaped prisoner.'

'You — helping an escaped prisoner? Who . . . ?'

'I'd rather not say, but it was someone who had a call on my loyalty. I did only what I considered right from my own point of view. I gave the man money. And by dirty thieving tricks this Peabody found out about it. He came here and threatened to see that the police got to know. He wanted twelve thousand as a first payment, and he didn't mean to stop there — so I disposed of him!'

Barry shook his head. 'Do you think it justified *those* measures?'

'Don't *you?*'

Barry got up, shaking his head: 'It isn't the course I'd have adopted myself. But now it's done, it's done.'

'It was the only course I could think of at the time. My mind was so muddled. You know yourself how I've been lately.'

'And that's been the cause of all your worry?'

Mills nodded, crossed to the window and stared out. He said, 'I think you understand, don't you? And you won't go to the police?'

'I gave my word — and I don't go back on it. I wouldn't have gone anyway, Jerry; I couldn't have gone, not remembering the years we've been firm friends. But — *murder!* Hell, I do think you might have drawn it *milder*, old man.'

'How *could* I draw it milder? It was the only way. It was either that, or pay him, or go to jail. I couldn't have gone on paying him, and I couldn't picture myself in jail — so it was *that*. Good God, Barry, you don't think I *liked* killing him do you?'

'Of course not. No, I imagine it *was* the only way.'

'Of course it was. It's exactly what *you'd* have done in the same circumstances. It wasn't murder — the man was the kind of slug that should have been exterminated long ago. I was only the unofficial executioner, that's all.'

'Look here, Jerry,' Barry replied. 'It's bad enough you having committed a murder — don't try to *justify* yourself into the bargain.'

'Shocked?' said Mills, the faint sneer returning.

'Did you expect me to take the news that my best friend had taken a human life, calmly?'

'He *wasn't* human. None of his kind *are*.'

'He was *alive* anyway — until last night!' said Barry.

'Yes, he was alive — but so is a beetle, or a snake, or a rat, alive — until someone exterminates them for the vermin they are. I can tell you, Barry, that I killed him without a twinge of conscience — without thinking about it at all. I knew I had to do

146

it when he first made his demands. That's why I elected to meet him in the spinney. I stabbed him just the way you'd put your foot on a cockroach!'

Barry murmured, 'I still find it a bit stiff to believe. I simply can't picture you as a — killer.'

Mills said, 'You'll get over it. I already have. How about lunching with me?'

Barry nodded. 'I'd like to. Now you've — well, got rid of this chappie — does it mean we can expect you to — to get back to normal again?'

Mills smiled and nodded. 'I hope so.' He wanted to smooth things over with Barry now. He didn't want Barry rushing off to the police with his story. It certainly would have been awkward.

But in spite of his calm appearance, as Barry had noticed, his nerves were leaping and his brain racing beneath the smile he wore. For now, night or day, everywhere he looked, every time his mind was off guard, he saw the little man in grey: figment of his distraught mind, and yet real enough to him. He was surprised that Barry didn't see him, standing in a shadowy corner, a dim grey outline in the darkness behind the curtains. It was hard to appreciate that he *himself* was creating that tenuous phantasm; that the little grey man was *only* in his *mind*. He had a feeling he could never again dodge that spectral face and figure — that the little man would go on waiting, waiting, for something which was inevitable, which *had* to happen. Soon.

They lunched and dined together, he and Barry — and the wraith.

Then Barry, who had not mentioned the murder again, suggested a run up to town and a visit to a good musical, to take Jerry's mind off 'things.'

Jerry agreed. He wanted badly to be alone, and yet he was hesitant to let Barry out of his sight. He had a feeling that at the first opportunity Barry would go to the police and put them on the right scent.

They took their box seats and settled down to enjoy the show. It was a first-class musical comedy, and for about twenty minutes it succeeded in driving other matters to the back of Mills's mind. But a chance remark on the stage brought things back to him vividly.

A remark about somebody 'seeing things.'

It was as easy as *that*. Suddenly, right before his eyes, the *little grey man was there*, where he was staring, on the *stage*. And he stayed there thereafter!

Mills had to loosen his collar. He did not hear the dialogue or see the action. He was only conscious of the grey man standing, waiting, everywhere he looked. He became fascinated. His eyes were glued to the stage.

Barry couldn't fail to notice his discomposure. At last he said, 'Don't you like it, old man?'

'Eh? What? Oh, yes — it's — very good. I — I need a drink, though. Don't — don't you come.'

He went out and through the bar and right out of the theatre. He couldn't have stayed there any longer. He wandered down Oxford Street blindly, hardly knowing where he was going. He kept walking, walking, crossing against the traffic at times, to wild curses from drivers.

Before him, always before him, went the little grey man. He didn't walk — he seemed to glide backwards so that his pale, emotionless eyes were fixed eternally on Mills.

Mills walked on, tramping through the rain which had begun to fall in a fine drizzle. He was without coat or hat, but he cared nothing for that. People were staring at the spectacle of a man in evening dress striding through the damp streets with a wild, fixed look in his eyes.

Once a policeman gazed at him curiously and seemed as if he would say something, but Mills was gone before he could make up his mind. Once a barrow hawker called, 'Watch where yer ruddy well goin', mate!'

Mills heard none of them; saw none of them. Engrossed in the image his crazed conscience had produced for him, he strode on heedlessly.

The rain came down more and more heavily, until at last he halted to take his bearings. He seemed to be somewhere in the Soho district. Exactly where, he had no idea. But on either side of him were restaurants purporting to be Greek and Italian.

There was a saloon bar on the corner.

150

He decided he needed a drink badly. He pushed open the doors and went in. The place was quiet; a few men smoked and drank in one corner. A youth and his foreign-looking girl leaned over the bar holding hands. The barman dispensed beer and smiles impartially. Halfway along the counter, seated on a high stool, was a woman. She was heavily painted, and her eyes were shadowed with blue. Her hair was a bottle shade of platinum; her teeth were quite obviously the work of some poor-class dentist. But she *was* a woman.

He walked along and took the seat beside her. He hardly noticed her until he was drinking the whisky he had ordered. Then she eyed his attire curiously and hopefully, and murmured, 'Say, you *are* wet, big boy!'

He didn't answer. He stared at her. The little grey man was behind her right shoulder, looking at him. The woman didn't know that, naturally. She went on, suggestively, 'You need warming up, Mister. Suppose you buy little Mamie a drink and we'll see what we can do.'

11

The Break

Why not, he thought, looking at her, and trying not to notice the little man in grey. Why not buy her drink and spend a little time in her company? At least it would help to take his mind off things — things he didn't want to think about.

'All right, Mamie. What're you drinking?'

'I never drink anything other than the best, big boy.'

'What's that?' he grunted.

'Beer.'

He laughed. 'Your clients don't like being rooked, do they? Well, tonight you can drink *gin* to your heart's content. Go ahead and order.'

She said, 'You mean that, Mister?'

'I mean it. Order.

She called to the barman: 'Got any vermouth, Slim?'

'Drain in the bottle, Mamie?'

'Make it gin an' it then. An' serve the gin in a separate glass to the vermouth.'

Mills said, 'Why that?'

'Listen, I used to be a barmaid. When you get the two mixed you can't see the gin they put in. This way you know what you're getting.'

'Know all the tricks, don't you?'

'You'll find out, big boy.'

He ordered another whisky neat, and drained it off. He looked at the wavering shape of the little grey man. He said, 'How 'bout you, frien'? Have a lil' drink?'

The little grey man remained expressionless, but Mamie looked over her shoulder, saw no one, then looked back at Mills. 'You all right? You haven't got the screamin' meemies by any chance, have you?'

'Mean you can't see my friend? Just behind you?'

She looked again. 'Say, you *are* nuts, big boy. Or are you jokin'?'

'Not at all. He follows me around . . . can't get rid of him. He won't give me any privacy.'

153

She looked a bit disturbed, and said, 'Are you on the *level?*'

'Why, do I look as though I'm standing in a hole?'

She laughed at that and said: 'Guess you *were* joking. You had me worried for a minute. I figured there was somebody there, following you.'

He smiled, but didn't try her any further. She ordered more gin and drank it. He ordered more neat whisky and drank that. The hands of the clock stole on towards ten. The barman bawled: 'Drink up now and show your backsides. Ain't you got any homes?' He switched out the light once or twice, and the customers began to trickle out.

Mills found the woman linking him. They were outside. She said, 'Coming along, big boy?'

He wasn't feeling any too good, but he said, 'Yes. Mind if Peeping Tom comes too?'

'Who's that?'

'That friend of mine.'

She grinned. 'Oh, sure. Let him come too. Let 'em all come.'

He said, 'How far?'

'Around the corner.'

It had stopped raining. The streets were black as black ivory.

They started walking . . .

★　★　★

Barry, unknown to his friend, had been following. He hadn't liked the look of Mills when he had left the box. Nor had he liked the fixed way Mills had stared at one spot on the stage. And he had decided it might be as well for him to keep an eye on Mills.

He had followed through the rain-soaked streets, getting as wet as Mills. His breath had caught in his throat once or twice when Mills had walked blindly across traffic-bound streets.

Then he had come to the saloon bar. He had followed Mills in and had sat to one side, round the corner of a piece of ornamental woodwork.

Mills was drinking heavily — too heavily. He was talking to a woman whose general style branded her as a street lady.

Barry found it hard to credit his eyes. Of all things, the very last thing Jerry — the Jerry *he* had known — might have been expected to do would have been to have any association with a woman of her type. But there he was — and obviously becoming quite friendly. They left at length when time was called, Mills carrying a half-bottle of whisky for which he paid three pounds.

Barry hated the idea of spying like this, but he was afraid to leave Mills alone. Heaven only knew what wretched depths of depravity his one-time friend had sunk to! He followed round the corner and watched them go into a shabby three-story house. He went into the porch, up the steps, and waited there.

He waited a long time; a very long time.

An hour ticked by on his wristwatch. He guessed they must be finishing the whisky.

At last there were sounds of movement from the stairs. He drew unobtrusively into the shadows. The woman came to the porch; she was supporting Mills. He was drunker than he'd ever been.

She said, 'There y'are, honey boy. Can you make it from here?'

Mills mumbled some inaudible reply. She steered him to the top step, where he stood swaying. She turned, leaving him there, and looked at Barry, standing in shadows. She ogled, 'Waiting for me, handsome?'

Barry said, 'I wouldn't wait for you if you were the last woman alive, sister. Get going.'

She snapped, 'Smart, aren't you?'

He said, 'Too smart to bother with your kind.'

She spat a filthy word at him and went back up the stairs.

Mills was lurching down the steps. He was halfway down when he missed a step, shot out head first, and caromed into the wet, glistening roadway. Barry said, 'Jerry!'

He went down, two steps at a time. Mills was sitting up with a dazed look, rubbing his head. He did not seem to be hurt. The old saying about a drunken man never hurting himself when he falls was in force. A relaxed body seldom takes the knock a keyed-up one does.

Barry helped him up. Mills peered at him through bleary eyes.

Barry said, 'You've had too much . . . '

'Wher'sh Mamie?' Mills wanted to know.

Barry grunted, 'Never mind Mamie. Have you got your wallet?'

Mills fumbled in his pocket. His face went blank. He said, 'Sh'funny.'

'I thought so. How much was in it?'

'About — about twenty pounds.'

'Hang on to these railings a minute. Don't move until I get back . . . understand?'

Mills got a grip on the railings. As Barry gained the top step he could hear him being good and sick. He went into the house and walked up the stairs. On the second landing he scanned the doors carefully. None of them indicated which one was occupied by Mamie. He shouted, 'Anybody home?'

Three doors opened. Three women popped out inelegant heads.

'I am, big boy.'

'Me too, sugar honey.'

'How 'bout lil' Rita?'

The second one was Mamie. He went into her room, pushing her back inside. The other doors closed. Now she got a look at him in the light, she snapped, 'Oh, you! You're the wise boy who was waiting in th' doorway, weren't you? Changed your mind about coming up?'

'I came for something that belongs to a friend of mine. You can hand it over peacefully or I'll call the police.'

She flushed. 'I don't know what you're getting at, Mister. I don't know any friend of yours.'

'He was just up here.'

She retorted, 'If you mean that drunken slob, I've got nothing belonging to him. Beat it, Mister, before I get annoyed.'

'I'm not going to argue. I want a wallet containing twenty pounds. Hand it over.'

She snorted, 'What's it to do with you? Your friend give me that. An' how'd I know he *is* your friend, anyway? How'd I know you aren't just trying to play some clever crooked game?'

159

'It needn't matter to you. Just give that wallet to me.'

She whined, 'Listen, big boy, a girl has to live, ain't she?'

'I don't see why. Anyway you'll make out without that. Still, if you'd rather I went for the police and brought them . . .'

She spat at him, 'All right, you — ! You know I can't afford to have flatties snoopin' round me. Here's the blasted wallet. An' tell your friend if he comes back here any time I'll give him a shiner!'

She forked down the top of her cheap print frock and threw the wallet to him. He opened it. The money was intact. He stripped off a pound note and threw it to her. Without another word he went out, shutting the door behind him.

He was almost at the steps when her door opened. Her head shot out. 'Hey, big boy — '

'Now what?' he grunted.

'You' won't tell the coppers, will you? You won't nark?'

'You don't have to worry. But you ought to watch your step.'

She slammed the door, and he went

downstairs. Mills was now flat out on the dirty wet roadway. He was groaning.

Barry jerked him to his feet and hoisted him along like a sack of coke to the corner. Mills kept twisting and falling. A policeman eyed them and said, 'Having any trouble, sir?' to Barry.

'If you could flag a taxi for me, officer . . . '

In a few minutes an empty taxi came rattling along. The P.C. waved a portentous arm, and the cabby braked.

Mills was crammed in, and Barry followed him. He slipped the P.C. a pound note. The P.C. said, 'Very kind of you, sir. Your friend'll be all right now. Good night.'

The cab drove away, Barry giving his own address. There was no need to take Mills to his *own* home in such a disgraceful state. It would only cause gossip amongst the servants.

As the cab rattled along he looked at the debauched spectacle of the man who had been his best friend, grimly.

'Jerry — can you hear me?'

'Yes'sh.'

'You understand what I'm saying?'

'Yes'sh, why?'

'This is the end, Jerry. I didn't think you'd sink as low as this. This time you've *really* torpedoed yourself. And you've no damned right — don't you care enough for Andrea to stop yourself playing *this* fool game?'

Jerry sneered, 'Haven you heard? Wedding'sh off! All off. Finished!'

Barry sat up straight. His heart was singing. He said, 'Is that the truth?'

'Didn't Andrea tell you?'

'No, she didn't. Perhaps she was too upset.'

'It'sh right enough. She left lash night for good. Donno where she went. Not comin' back.'

Barry said, 'I'm glad to hear it. But anyway we're through, Jerry, and from here on you can handle your own troubles.'

'Thash whad I want. You haven't been any help anyway.'

There was a silence; then Mills muttered: 'I — I feel — shick!'

'I'm not surprised. You look it.'

'My head — my head'sh goin' roun' . . .'

He suddenly flopped sideways against Barry, completely out. He lay like that, and was still like that when the cab screeched up outside Barry's apartments.

The cabby got out and gave Barry a hand. He grinned. 'What happened to him? He fall in a barrel of whisky?'

'Something of the kind.'

'He sure smells like it. I ain't smelled anything like that since I worked for Black and White.'

They dumped Jerry on the settee, and Barry gave the driver a handsome tip. The driver turned to go. Barry bent over Mills.

Mills had his *mouth open* — that was what gave Barry the sudden *shock*.

Percival came in from his room in a dressing gown. Barry snapped, 'Percival — keep Mister Mills here at all costs, until I get back.'

'Keep him *here*, sir?'

'Yes. Don't let him go, even if you have to *hit* him with something.'

'But sir — we are not very adequate when it comes to the art of fisticuffs.'

'Then use the poker. But hold him!'

He left Percival standing scratching his head by the senseless form of Mills. He raced down the stairs again and was in time to catch the cabby just pulling away. He tumbled in and gave an address.

It was a long ride, taking the best part of an hour, and all the way he was in a fidget of impatience. At last they drew up and the cabby said, 'Here y'are, sir. Thank you, sir.'

'Wait here a minute — may need you again.'

He knocked at the door of the large house at which they had drawn up. A glance at his wristwatch told him it was after eleven. He hammered hard, then waited. After about five minutes he heard steps. Slow steps. The door opened cautiously. Andrea looked out.

'Andrea — it's important that I see you now — at once.'

She was in a négligée and nightgown. But he hardly noticed her beauty. He went on, 'It's about — Jerry.'

Instantly she nodded. 'Come inside, Barry. Be quiet — Aunt Amy's in bed, and I'd hate her to hear us talking and investigate. She'd die of apoplexy on the spot!'

She took him into a sitting room, furnished in a rather Mid-Victorian fashion, with bric-a-brac and well-stuffed antimacassars. She indicated a seat and said, 'What about Jerry, Barry? Nothing's happened to him — has it?'

'Nothing you need to worry yourself about — yet. But I've found something out. Listen, Andrea — do you remember last year, when Jerry went along to have a *gold tooth* to replace the back one that he'd lost?'

She hesitated a moment: 'I — oh, yes. I remember.'

'He *did* have it fitted, didn't he?'

'Why yes. He showed it to me when he came back.'

Barry said, 'Then you'd better prepare yourself for a shock. Jerry got drunk tonight — he flopped out. And while I was looking him over, I happened to notice he *hadn't any gold teeth in his head!*'

'Barry — *no*! It's impossible.'

Barry took her hand gently. 'It's true. I've thought for a long time now that

Jerry wasn't himself. And he isn't himself. It isn't just mental — he must be *another* man!'

A sudden light of understanding flashed into her eyes. She clutched his hand tight. Her voice was strained. 'Barry — when he made that — that trip to Marseilles!'

'What about it?'

'He — he went to take money to — to his twin brother, Harold. Harold had escaped from the Foreign Legion!'

Barry's face was suddenly white. He said, '*God!*'

She almost whispered, 'Barry — you don't think . . . ?'

He said slowly, 'I don't know, Andrea. But I'm afraid we have to have proof — after all, Jerry may have had the gold tooth replaced with a porcelain one. Gold isn't fashionable any longer.'

'He might have. How can you find out?'

'His dentist. And I'm going to find out tonight! Who is his dentist? Do you know?'

She told him, and found a telephone directory. He started skimming through

166

the names. There was a step behind them, and they both spun round. Aunt Amy had materialised. She was poised in the doorway with a look of inexpressive horror on her angular countenance. She was favouring woollen nightwear with a discreet bathrobe over it. A suggestion of red wool peeped coyly from under her robe. She was regarding him with a shocked, stern glare from behind her rimless pince-nez.

'So this — *this*,' she thundered, 'is what I find taking place — *in my own home*!'

She advanced a step and hissed, 'Young man, how dare you! How *dare* you, I say?'

12

Nemesis

Barry, meanwhile, had found the address of the dentist. He scribbled it hastily on a piece of paper, then faced the wrathful Aunt Amy, who was undoubtedly upon the verge of a telling denunciation. She had just opened her mouth to give vent to her feelings on the matter of finding a presentable young man with her favourite niece in a state of undress, in her own house in the late hours, when Barry brushed rudely past her.

'Sorry, Aunt Amy,' he grunted familiarly. 'In a hurry and all that. Andrea, darling, you explain to your Aunt — ask her to come up and see my *etchings* sometime.'

Aunt Amy barked, 'Upon my soul!'

'Then,' continued Barry, 'get your togs and dash over to my apartments. You may as well be in at the showdown, I suppose.'

He rushed through the doorway and was gone.

The cab was still waiting. And now he was on the trail at last, Barry meant to finish the affair that very night. If Jerry was an impostor, the sooner he was exposed the better for all concerned.

The cab rushed him back to the West End; he found the address he wanted, hopped out, and told the driver to wait again.

He rung the night bell, and a middle-aged gentleman in carpet slippers answered the door.

'I'm awfully sorry to worry you at this hour, sir,' Barry told him. 'But my business is rather urgent. I presume you're the dentist who attends to Gerald Mills?'

The man nodded. 'I am Mister Mills's dental surgeon, yes.'

'Then perhaps you could tell me if Mr. Mills had a gold tooth fitted about a year ago?'

'That's rather a strange question, young man. On what authority do you come asking these questions?'

'On my own authority. I am forced to

believe that, in some way, an impostor has stepped into Mr. Mills's shoes.'

'An impostor? But that's fantastic — '

'Mr. Mills had a twin brother. He left the country almost six years ago after some — unpleasantness . . . '

'I recall the man you mean. A shiftless ne'er-do-well.'

'I believe that the man who now claims to be Gerald Mills is none other than his brother, Harold. You, as a dentist, can prove the true identity of Mr. Mills, can't you?'

'Why, yes. But it's rather late . . . '

'But the matter is important. Now is the time to put it to the test, whilst the man is off guard. He's at my apartments, drunk and sleeping.'

'You wish me to go with you?'

'I would be grateful, sir.'

The dentist nodded and said, 'You will have to wait until I have collected some notes from my files. My memory is hardly good enough to recall the structure of Mr. Mills's molars from memory. Although I do have recollections of fitting him with a rear gold molar about the time you say.'

'And he did not have it changed for a

porcelain type later?'

'Not with me.'

He hurried away to don his street clothes and collect the notes he had mentioned. Within ten minutes he was ready to accompany Barry.

The taxi hurried away along the damp streets once more, bringing the denouement ever nearer.

★   ★   ★

Andrea Marsh drew her sleek roadster into the kerb outside the building wherein was Barry's apartment. She got out and hurried into the block. No one was about — the lift was waiting idly at the ground floor. She stepped into it, thumbed the buttons and shot up. At Barry's floor she got off and looked down towards the entrance to his flat.

The door was closed. There was no sign of movement, no sign of life. She hurried along and pressed the bell.

The door opened and Percival, the valet, looked out at her. But not the usually immaculate Percival she knew. This one spotted a multi-coloured swollen eye and a burst nose. His dressing gown was smeared with blood and his hands dithered as they wiped industriously at his blood-stained chin.

'*Percival!* What . . . ?'

'I told the master I was unused to fisticuffs, Miss,' said Percival mournfully. 'Mr. Mills woke up whilst we were in the kitchen preparing a cup of coffee — he appeared to be in a very bad temper, and insisted on leaving to return home. When we told him we considered he was in no condition to return anywhere, Miss, he became extremely vulgar in his language. He — ' continued Percival, plaintively: 'Hurt our *feelings!* Yes, indeed.'

'And then . . . ?'

'We insisted upon his remaining. At which point he struck us boisterously upon the nose. And then, when we attempted to grapple, he stamped on our corn and smote us in the optic. We fell like Lucifer, son of the morning, from our high estate, Miss, and when we crawled to our feet he had gone!'

She said, 'Where is Mr. Barry?'

'He has not yet returned — and,' continued Percival, with an injured look, 'When he does so we shall tender our month's resignation. We are unaccustomed to brawling, Miss.'

At that moment the lift whizzed down again, and whizzed up with Barry and the dentist in it. They hurried towards the apartment and pulled up short at the sight of Percival. Barry said:

'*Perce* — *! Good God, man*, you didn't let him *go?*'

'I did not, sir. He attacked us most nefariously, and we had no alternative.'

'You — you didn't tell him I suspected anything, though?'

'I did not *know* that you suspected anything, sir. I appear to be merely the sparring partner here — and such being the case I desire to tender my resignation, to take effect from . . . '

Barry grinned. 'How many times is that you've resigned *this year*, Perce? Now don't look so upset — go and get some steak from the larder for that eye, and I'll see you when I get back. How long has Mills been gone?'

'About fifteen minutes, sir.'

Barry nodded. 'Good. Then we'll get off over to his home. No reason he should suspect anything . . . '

★ ★ ★

Mills lolled drunkenly in the library, the window open to admit air. He was sitting behind his desk, head on hands. He dared not look up — he knew the little grey man would be there. In fact, now his drunkenness was beginning to wear off, the grey man was plainer every time he looked up. Still without an expression, still wooden and motionless.

He heard the sound of a car roar up in the drive. He stared dumbly at the library door.

Suddenly it burst open, and Barry, Andrea, and a man he had never seen before stepped in.

Mills held himself steady and rasped, 'What the hell is *this?*'

'It isn't a social call, Mills,' stated Barry grimly.

'Get out of here! I've finished with you

174

and Andrea, I've made that plain. Why can't you leave me alone? And who the devil is that with you?'

'You don't know this man?'

'Should I?'

'You should. You should know him quite well!'

'I can't think clearly now. Leave me alone — '

Barry said quietly, 'I'm afraid that's impossible — *Harold*!'

Mills gripped tighter to the edge of the desk. He said, 'You don't know what you're saying! What do you mean — Harold?'

'You *are* Harold Mills, aren't you?'

'You fool, have you gone mad? You know damn well I'm Jerry Mills!'

'I know nothing of the kind. I believe you're Harold Mills. What you've done with Jerry I don't know — but I mean to find out!'

'By God,' shouted Mills, half rising. 'I'll have you in court for this, Arnton! How dare you . . . '

'You claim you *are* Jerry, then?'

'Of course I claim I'm Jerry!'

'Then you can't have any objection to

putting it to the test?'

Mills's eyes shifted from one to the other. He said, 'How can you do that?'

'Quite easily. Mr. Mills, meet the man you should have known but didn't — *your dental surgeon*, Mr. Potter!'

Potter stepped forward and stared at Mills. Mills had gone pale. His fingers dropped away from the desk top. He whispered, 'What can *he* prove?'

Potter said, 'A look at the inside of your mouth will suffice to prove your identity, Mr. Mills. Gerald Mills has a false gold tooth.'

A taut smile crossed Mills's lips suddenly. He stood up and said, 'I see. That, of course, would be *conclusive* proof. But if I object to this test?'

Barry snapped, 'You won't be *permitted* to object!'

Mills nodded and said, 'Thank you. That's all I need to know. You are right, gentlemen — *I have no false tooth in my head*. And I am *Harold Mills*!'

Barry started forward — then stopped.

Mills had lifted his right hand from under cover of the desk. In it he held a small revolver he had taken from the drawer, and although the hand was wavering, the range was far too short for him to miss.

'Yes, I am Harold Mills,' he said again. 'The teeth would prove it beyond doubt. There is also another matter — a matter of the scars on my back, left there by a flogging! I got that in the Legion — but you wouldn't know about the Legion.'

Barry said, 'What have you done with — Jerry?'

Mills shrugged, holding the gun steady. 'Jerry? A fool — a noble fool — but still a fool! I murdered him!'

Andrea gave a tiny cry, and Barry slipped an arm about her to save her from falling. Potter was trembling at the knees. Mills went on, 'It surprised me that you didn't suspect something much sooner than this. It was a far harder thing to impersonate Jerry than I had thought. Possibly because our natures differed so much. And then there was the matter of Peabody, who knew about it all. It meant *he* had to be killed too — and that shook me up a little. I had intended to put my old ways right behind me — didn't realise how impossible that was going to be.

'There were the dreams I had, too, and the apparition which my own mental stress conjured up. You know the little *grey* man. He was *here* until you burst in — now, due to the excitement I expect, he's gone again.

'I was prepared for this emergency. When my plans didn't work so well as I had hoped, I never let myself forget that at any moment the game might be up. It is up, now.

'I have in this drawer a neat paper packet. It contains the twelve thousand pounds which was meant for Peabody, if I had failed to kill him that night.'

He slid the money inside his coat as he spoke. He went on, 'Enough to pay for an unofficial passage on some ocean-going tramp, whose skipper would not be too scrupulous. Enough to make a fresh start in some country where I cannot be traced, and where I may be able to lose this damned vision that haunts me. Mr. Potter, you must have had many people at your mercy in the chair before today, mustn't you? How does it feel to be at the absolute mercy of someone *else?*'

Potter gulped.

'You don't like it? You love life, eh? Then you will do as I advise, at once, or I will not hesitate to shoot you down. Take the cords from these curtains — quickly.'

Potter obeyed tremulously.

'Good. Now bind Arnton and the girl by the wrists . . . but keep behind them, out of the way. Hurry, man!'

There was nothing else to be done. Potter fumbled and flummoxed, but at last the wrists of the girl and the man were tied.

Mills said, 'Excellent. I see you were wary enough to make a good job of it. That is well from your point of view. Now take the two covers from those cushions . . . gag them . . .'

Potter did that also. Mills continued, 'There is a large and airy cupboard on that side of the room. Open it, push these two inside, then lock it and bring the key to me. Hurry.'

Potter steered the helpless pair towards the cupboard, put them inside, locked the door, and came back to Mills. Mills took the key from him and murmured, 'Thank you. And now goodbye, Mister Potter. You've been very useful — if I ever need any teeth extracting I'll come to *you!*'

The reversed gun crushed down on top of Potter's skull, and the dentist flopped down onto the floor without a groan.

Mills wasted no time. He did not even pause for coat and hat. Already the girl and Barry were banging their feet on the door of the cupboard, and this would soon bring the servants to investigate.

He slid the gun into his pocket and ran through the open French window. Outside was a taxi, and just beyond it Andrea's car. He raced by the astonished taxi driver and climbed into the car. He started up.

His foot went hard down the second he gained the road. His plan was to put as great a distance as possible between himself and the people who knew his secret, then to dump the car and work his way towards the docks where he might contact a suitable hideout until he was able to arrange an illegal passage from the country.

He covered the ground at a great rate, his path leading him upwards . . .

He was on a narrow, winding road, hardly more than a rough track running up the side of a hill. To the right, guarded only by a clumsy wooden fence, was a sheer drop of hundreds of feet. He coaxed still more speed from the car. It was running beautifully, the sound of its motors a dull roar on the quiet night air.

And then he saw *the little man!*

This time in front of him, before his eyes, beyond the windshield! About him was a haze, making everything indistinct and vague.

He became aware of the sharp, shooting pain in his head, and found his hands had developed a sudden inability to feel, to obey the orders his brain flashed to them. The pain in his head grew worse — he wondered if this was the mental breakdown prophesied by the old psychiatrist, brought on by the recent strain of events.

The little grey man was growing plainer every minute. He still showed a bland, wooden countenance.

Mills made a tremendous effort to bring the car back into control, to make the hands which gripped the wheel obey his bidding. But it was useless. The messages his confused brain flashed through seemed to dissolve the moment he had thought them, without having any effect upon the hands at all. He watched the hands fascinatedly, trying to ignore the fierce throbbing ache in his skull. They were like the hands of a stranger, not connected with him at all. He seemed to be watching someone else careering along madly in a car they could no longer control.

He tore his eyes up again and saw the little man in grey. He felt the wheels suddenly skidding against empty air, and for a brief second he saw down into the long, bone-breaking drop below.

Then the car was plunging, plunging, and his hands came up to his eyes — and before they covered them, he knew death had come!

The little man in grey was there, even though Mills had covered his eyes — and now, at the last, his waiting was done. He was smiling . . .

The car plunged like a spent rocket into the drop. A shrill, terrified scream floated back, and then was cut short by the mighty thundering crash as the car hit the ground.

A sheet of orange flame swept, roaring, into the night.

★ ★ ★

Barry came into the bedroom and eyed Andrea Arnton, almost drooling at the lips. She was in a filmy nightgown, in bed. He said, 'How does it feel being a female wolf, sweetheart?'

'I'll let you know when the honeymoon's over.' She gazed curiously at the package he was carrying and said, 'Present?'

He placed the package in the fireplace and touched a match to it. She said, 'Barry, what on earth *is* that?'

'Those? Oh, just my *etchings*. I don't *need* 'em any longer, darling!'

And she murmured, just before he kissed her, 'You'd better *not*, either!'

THE END

We do hope that you have enjoyed reading this large print book.

Did you know that all of our titles are available for purchase?

We publish a wide range of high quality large print books including:
Romances, Mysteries, Classics General Fiction Non Fiction and Westerns

Special interest titles available in large print are:
The Little Oxford Dictionary Music Book, Song Book Hymn Book, Service Book

Also available from us courtesy of Oxford University Press:
Young Readers' Dictionary (large print edition) Young Readers' Thesaurus (large print edition)

For further information or a free brochure, please contact us at:
Ulverscroft Large Print Books Ltd., The Green, Bradgate Road, Anstey, Leicester, LE7 7FU, England. Tel: (00 44) 0116 236 4325 **Fax:** (00 44) 0116 234 0205

THE CHAINED MAN
AND OTHER STORIES

Gerald Verner

When a band of stranded Christmas travellers is forced to spend the night in an isolated local pub called the Chained Man, the last thing they expect is murder in their midst . . . Lattimer Shrive puts his amazing powers of detection and deduction to work to solve three seemingly inexplicable cases . . . And a real murder on national radio proves surprisingly tricky to solve. These five detective stories by Gerald Verner will baffle and entertain in equal measure.

THE DARCKMOOR DEMON AND OTHER ENIGMAS

John Light

Who or what is responsible for the eerie howling from the night-darkened fells that disturbs the inhabitants of Darckmoor? Is there malice at work in the world of small presses? Why is there an eight-foot-high toadstool on the back of a truck speeding along a remote byway? When a new statue by a reclusive artist is displayed in a small gallery in London's East End, is it the beginning of something bigger? And what is the cause of the sorrowful single-mindedness of the long-term resident of an old-fashioned hotel?